To Nic...

BOULEVARD
BEAUSÉJOUR

With best wishes

Jane Foster

Palm Beach   May 1st 2017

JANEDEMORETFOSTER@GMAIL .

BOULEVARD BEAUSÉJOUR

A NOVEL BY FOSTER AND YELLAND

Green Dragon Books
Palm Beach, FL, USA

BOULEVARD BEAUSÉJOUR

A Green Dragon Publishing Group Publication

Green Dragon Publishing
P.O. Box 1608
Lake Worth, FL 33460
http://www.greendragonbooks.com
info@greendragonbooks.com

Printed in the United States of America and the United Kingdom

ISBN (Paperback) 978-1-62386-050-9
ISBN (e-book) 978-1-62386-051-6

Library of Congress Cataloging-in-Publication Data Control # Available

DEDICATION
To our treasures
Augusta, Eleanor, Giraud, Jack, Rob and Samuel

ACKNOWLEDGEMENTS

We want to express our heartfelt gratitude
to all our family and friends who have read
and commented on numerous drafts.
Very special thanks go to the meticulous and congenial
Richard Yelland for his editing par excellence,
and to the incomparable Bernadette Barbier.
And we are indebted to the Paris writers' group
so skilfully managed by Gretel Furner,
without whom we would never have met.

CHAPTER 1

Andrew Harris flinched as his bald spot was hit. In no mood for sabotage, he lashed out and managed to tear off a few green tips from the overhanging cedar branch. Now, his trench coat was ripped and his remaining hair was thoroughly soaked, thanks to a few fat raindrops. Andy was upset and in need of a rest.

"April in Paris. Great. And it hasn't rained for hours," he muttered. Then, as an afterthought, he added, "But I guess this beats Alice getting *her* hair wet."

Bedraggled, he stood swaying a little, in front of an elegant apartment building on Boulevard Beauséjour. It was time to take on the door.

Andrew Harris, former New York art critic and current trailing spouse, had been living in Paris for almost three months, but still couldn't remember the correct code for his building having pressed so many near misses. He tried 17-A-76. No good. Then 71-A-67, no good, either. "Damn and more damn," he mumbled as he fumbled to unlock his phone to find the code, but the phone was new and its clever code eluded him, as well. Back to the door. 17-B-67. The door opened, and there stood the live-in landlady, Brigitte Barbier, with Romeo, her brown basset hound at her heel. She was wearing platform shoes and a weary look of disapproval.

"*Bonjour*, Monsieur 'Arreese. All wet and forgetting zuh code encore? I write it for you." She took out a scrap of paper from her pocket with the numbers written on it. "Voila. 11-A-77. *Bonne journée, monsieur.*" She made 'good day, sir' sound like the beginning of an ancient incantation.

"*Merci*, Madame," Andy said loudly, and then lowering his voice as he stumbled through the door, continued, "for having X-ray eyes and always knowing every single little thing about every single little soul in your building." Andy turned and bowed in an exaggerated Hollywood manner waving the scrap of paper.

"My duty and honor, monsieur." She managed to emphasize the 'h' in honor. Did he detect a flicker of a smile?

Andy wobbled further into the building and produced the heavily laden key ring from his pocket. He managed to insert the correct large key into the next barrier between himself and his apartment. He did this fluidly even under the scrutiny of Madame Barbier and Romeo. He then forced his six-foot-four frame into the tiny wood-paneled elevator and poked the fifth floor button. The spacious, the silent, the welcoming fifth floor.

While rising in the elevator, he commenced rehearsing in his head the telephone conversation he would soon be having with his twin brother. "So," he said silently. "This morning I'm trying to sleep off a little hangover, and my think-tank-thinker wife starts screaming about her hair. This has been going on for weeks now. What am I supposed to do about her hair? Now, I may not be clear on all my duties as a trailing spouse - that quaint little ex-pat term for the unemployed half of a couple here in France, in case you didn't know exactly what I am now. But, lemme tell you what, I'm positive hair is not one of them. She says, 'It's impossible.' She says, 'It's willful.' She says, 'It shouldn't be allowed out.'"

The elevator stopped. Andy fought with its two heavy doors. The first required sliding from left to right, the second, pushing away from him. Two more keys and finally he opened his own front door. Arms raised in victory, he stepped into the echoing hall.

Black and white marble squares covered the floor. On the freshly painted bare white walls were holes left from the previous tenants' sconces, looking like missing teeth in a beauty queen. Illuminated by three naked light bulbs dangling from the ceiling, the hall said it all.

Andy dropped his trench coat on the floor and pulled out his wallet. He would show them, that Madame Barbier and Romeo. He would keep this special code of theirs at the ready. He frowned, concentrating on the contents of his wallet. Shuffling through cards and currency, he was surprised to find several identical scraps, all with the same sequence of numbers. Next time, he thought, narrowing his eyes.

Going into the living room, Andy plunked himself down on one of the pair of throne-like chairs - a flea market find the first weekend they'd arrived. So far this was the only furniture in the large, paneled room, but in compliance with one of many French rules, most of the room was covered with a carpet. Andy promised himself he would use the industrial sized Hoover, left by the prior tenant, on this multi-colored monster soon. His wife should not be obliged to return to a slovenly household after a day of thinking.

Andy patted himself down and pulled out his phone. He closed one eye and took a closer look. Stabbing at the screen with his index finger did not produce the desired result. "Oooh, the post-its," he groaned. Andy struggled to his feet and went to the secret code-hiding place. He removed the hand towel covering the box which served as his bedside table and moved the map of Paris, which neatly covered the string of scribbled numbers. God, Alice would have a fit if she saw this homeland security breach jackpot. Finally, he opened his phone and speed-dialed Billy. He checked his watch. Five p.m. Paris; ten a.m. Texas. He reached a recording and waited for the beep.

"Say, Billy-Bob. Doesn't Alice's hair always look great? We're having a crisis here. Call me back."

Andy went into the bedroom, kicked off his shoes and fell into the unmade bed, crossed his ankles, put his hands behind his head and surveyed his domain. The door to Alice's walk-in closet was closed. But he knew behind that door every single item was perfectly ordered and color-coded. Each shoe, glove and sock had its mate and every hanger matched. It had taken a great deal of time and energy to make this happen. Andy's closet door was wide open and did not contain matching hangers.

His closets had always been a mess, and Alice never said a negative word about it. Andy's mind drifted back to Furnald Hall and his undergraduate days at Columbia. He pictured Alice sitting primly in the front row of their Intellectual Property class, Junior year. She took his breath away. Five-five, with a perfect body and a kind of unsettling beauty. Even her feet were beautiful, and while no one could accuse Alice of being an athlete, she was graceful. "Probably all that ballet," he reasoned, nodding his head.

Everyone responded to Alice's beauty except Alice herself. For a woman with such an astounding I.Q, she could be amazingly obtuse at times. Andy chuckled recalling how shocked she'd been when he'd asked to borrow her notes on Intellectual Property. And how proud she was when he got into NYU's Institute of Fine Arts. He thought of the little apartment they'd shared on West 92nd Street after graduation, and his heart swelled when he remembered how she looked on their wedding day. Andy's eyes were beginning to sting.

The phone rang. "Why are we talking about Alice's hair?" It was Billy.

Andy turned off the maudlin tears and sat up. "All of a sudden, it's outrageously important to her. Way up there, on the level with her job or something. And now she's started to thread her fingers through it and raise it from her scalp. It's terrible. Distorting. Then she starts questioning me. Like, 'What am I supposed to do with this hair? Wake up, Andrew, and answer me.'" Andy had used that high squeaky voice he saved for imitating Alice behind her back. Feeling disloyal, he dropped it and said, "It's just not like her."

"Actually, it is like her. Think about it, bro. This is your opportunity. Find her a hairdresser. They're like shrinks. Get her some help. She's had a hard time."

Andy agreed. "You're right. Going right now. Got to save Alice."

He cut the connection and slowly heaved himself off the bed, held on to the door handle to ease the dizziness and made his way into the tiny kitchen. He opened the fridge, reached for a Coke and slugged it back before shrugging on his ripped coat to go out. Only a couple of Cokes left. He made a mental note to replenish the supply. Quite a few mental notes littered his brain, some dating back quite a long time.

He bypassed several hairdressers thinking they weren't hip enough, more like hip-replacement, actually. Then he stopped in front of Patrick Rolland's and looked through the large plate glass window. Energetic grooming of both men and women was going on. He spotted the impresario himself and boldly walked in. He'd found his man.

The sum total of Andy's French language skills allowed him to say *"Bonjour, Madame (or Monsieur). Je suis Andy. Je suis American. Excusez-moi de ne pas parler français. Parlez-vous anglais?"* He said this to everyone, all day long. He said it respectfully, with humility in his irresistible Texas accent, which won him many friends. These simple words worked nearly every time, this time included. He said it standing in the middle of the salon. And for a second it felt like time stood still as clients, colorists, manicurists and make-up artists all turned to this big, handsome thirty-something Texan and waited for whatever was going to happen next.

"'Allo, Handy. I'm Patrick Rolland. Be welcome. What can I do?" Patrick was a tall man of forty-five with wavy brown hair adjusting to its first streaks of silver. He was fit, but not gym-rat fit, and today Lulu, his Jack Russell terrier, was wearing her purple ribbon to match Patrick's left sock. His right sock was turquoise, as were the shoelaces on his expensive black brogues.

Andy had never had his hair washed or blown dry by someone else before, but he figured there was no time like the present. Patrick walked Andy off to a bar of sinks and introduced him to Giselle, a diminutive lady in black who was well past retirement age. As Andy slid back and allowed his head to weigh heavily in Giselle's capable hands, her husky voice intoned the initial bars of "Somewhere Over the Rainbow". While she shampooed and massaged Andy, the corny lyrics somehow washed his anxieties down the drain. The beribboned Lulu had followed Andy to the sink and had remained by his side, alerting Patrick and Giselle to the fact that here sat a man in crisis.

Andy left the salon believing that everything would be all right. Besides having much improved hair, he had an official letter welcoming Alice to Patrick Rolland Coiffeur, where she now had unlimited access to all of their services, compliments of her concerned and adoring husband.

That evening, Alice arrived home a little after seven. She put her briefcase on the marble floor and carefully hung her coat in the hall closet. "Hi, honey, I'm home," she quipped, as usual. For someone with an advanced degree in Philosophy - more specifically, twin doctorates in Decision Theory and Rational Choice - Alice had a pretty good sense of humor. Andy pretended he thought this particular greeting was funny, but it had been going on now every weekday since arriving in Paris.

Alice looked like she didn't have a thought in her blond head. She wore a pink angora sweater with a gray lace skirt and dangerous Louboutins on her size six feet. Andy marveled at her contradictions as he brought a tray with the fixings for champagne cocktails into the living room. He placed it carefully on the boxes that served as a coffee table, bent down and kissed the back of her neck. They'd been too busy becoming Parisians to bother with details like unpacking and buying furniture. Who needed lamps and tables when there were light bulbs and serviceable boxes already in place?

Presenting Alice with the gift certificate, Andy sipped his cocktail while he waited for her over-reaction. Alice was the over-reactive type and today, as usual, he had no idea what to expect.

Alice danced around him. "Why are you dancing, Alice?" Andy swallowed the rest of his cocktail and steeled himself.

"I'm so relieved." She sang. "Oh, Andrew, you have listened to me and found an answer. I'm the luckiest woman in the whole wide world to have such a sensitive and handsome and smart and thoughtful husband." Andy poured them both another cocktail and regaled her with the story of his first blow-dry. Alice laughed and ruffled his hair.

"You look fantastic with your hair all fluffy, Andrew. We should celebrate and go to La Rotonde for dinner. But promise me, you won't let Damien bring out your computer."

Andy's computer was at La Rotonde because he had not yet been successful in having WiFi installed in their apartment. French WiFi providers had resisted his charm and were not playing ball with a non-French speaker, even if he freely admitted this defect in his education. He had an amicable arrangement with the restaurant where he had a cheeseburger and French fries every day for lunch, and the manager kept his computer locked in the office and brought it to him whenever he came in. Andy spent most weekday mornings there, arriving for coffee around nine. All his best weekday French friends worked at La Rotonde. Some days he spent the whole day there, and on others he left right after an early lunch, not to return until six.

"I promise I won't ask for my laptop. The special today is lamb chops. I almost didn't have a cheeseburger for lunch because they looked so good, but I stayed pure."

"I don't know why you think it's so important to eat the same darn lunch every day, year in, year out."

"It's the principle of the thing, darlin'. I'm staying true to my cattle ranching roots, and I definitely don't want to be another international sushi-eater. In New York people came to respect me for my cheeseburgers."

"Not respect, Andrew. Accept."

"In New York, acceptance is respect."

"Do you miss it?"

"Miss what?"

"Working at *Cool* and going to all the art openings?"

"Nope. I wouldn't trade my days at La Rotonde for all the art in New York. I'd much rather be your trailing spouse. Anyway, that was over while you were still teaching at Columbia."

"I'm just wondering...."

Andy held up the palm of his hand. "Please. Let's not go there." He went back into the hall and picked his coat up off the floor. In truth, Andy missed the secret funding and the black American Express card that was never really his. Lamenting his spendthrift ways, he thought back on investments he should have made.

At La Rotonde, Gregory welcomed Andy and Alice warmly, but with surprise. "If I'd known you were coming, I'd have had your table waiting for you, but Neil will take you to the curved banquette where you can sit side-by-side."

With the coffee and cognac before them Alice moved closer to Andy and slipped her arm through his. "I know you don't like my asking but I need to make sure you're happy here without a job."

"Darlin', I'm not worried. Something'll surface soon." Andy wanted to change the subject but Alice spoke again before he had the chance.

"I couldn't be at Phaye analyzing rational decision making all day long, if I didn't have the luxury of you taking care of everything for me. I certainly don't have any talent for finances. And, anyway, we're both doing it as Aristotle said, 'Love is a single soul inhabiting two bodies.'"

The soft lights played off the mirrors, jazz whispered in the background, and Alice, unlike Andy, thought all was well with the world.

CHAPTER 2

Alice left the apartment early the next morning, clutching Patrick Rolland's address. She arrived as Patrick was opening the heavy glass door to the salon. From the way Andy had described her, he knew right away she was Alice and Lulu knew, too.

"*Bonjour, Madame 'Arreese*. Be welcome. What can I do?"

"*Bonjour, monsieur*. I'm here for a blow dry, if you can take me right away."

"I give you a little trim, *madame*?" Patrick appreciated Alice's kick-ass Alexis Mabille suit and Caroline Abram shades. Of course, he noticed she was gorgeous, but everyone noticed that. Of course she noticed his socks, but everyone noticed them. Today one sock was fuschia, and the shoelaces and other sock were apple green, as was Lulu's ribbon. Alice didn't know what to say in either English or French.

"I don't know about the trim, *monsieur*. My hair sort of hurts. Do you know what I mean?"

Patrick held one or two strands of Alice's limp hair. "Madame, your hair is dying of thirst. *Naturellement*, it hurts. We give it a nice drink. Hydration therapy. That should make it feel better."

This guy's brilliant, thought Alice, of course, that's what's been wrong all these months. Dehydration.

Alice's hair was still long when she left the salon, but she had an appointment for later in the week and was thrilled that her hair did, indeed, feel better. It looked better, too. Alice kissed both of Patrick's cheeks before she left for work with a spring in her step.

The Phaye Institute was housed in an 18th century chateau on the other side of the Jardin du Ranelagh from the Harris's apartment. When they arrived in February, Andy and Alice could see the chateau through the leafless trees, but now it was being obscured as spring advanced. Each day at the Institute was different. This was a big change for Alice from her predictable ivory tower life at Columbia University, where first as a teaching assistant, then as an assistant professor, she enjoyed a strict sense of order. Each class having its special room, its tight syllabus and its scheduled students gave Alice the routine she'd always craved.

Alice had been invited to Phaye to provide her insight and expertise to the broad range of projects the Institute supported around the globe. Her boss, Henri Frazier, first met Alice in California at a TED conference. She was one of the speakers, and he watched her being filmed. Henri was a polished, middle-aged, well-educated Frenchman originally from Bordeaux who couldn't believe his eyes and ears. Alice was too beautiful and too smart, and try as he might, he couldn't get her out of his mind. The Phaye Institute did not really need an in-house philosopher, but a few months later, after reading one of her publications on Rational Choice, Henri hired her anyway. A special position for someone with precisely her academic background and renowned organizational skills became available. His letter offering this tailor-made career change arrived the same week that Andy received some rather unflattering press. The timing was perfect for a geographical relief.

The sheer beauty of her new work environment was inspirational to Alice. The Chateau was built long before Paris expanded to absorb it, and although it no longer had a park, it still had a small garden and retained its original paneling, molding and floors. Alice loved the proportions of her office; she said she could think better in this cube-shaped room. Now, almost three months in, she was beginning to relax and find her way around Paris, only occasionally admitting to herself that she missed the strict routine of academia.

She sometimes wondered about this switching of roles in her marriage as well. Andy had been the one with the glamour-job in New York, and she was the dreary assistant philosophy professor. Now.... What was Andrew now? She wasn't really sure whether Andy had resigned or was fired from *Cool*. He had told her not to worry about the money since he had high hopes that any day now on family land back in Texas cattle ranching would turn into oil ranching.

Alice loved Andy with her whole heart, although she couldn't imagine what he did all day. She felt reassured when he said it was not really that different to what he had done in New York and believed him when he said he was happy to be in Paris.

"Alice, your hair. You look sublime," Yvette said, handing over a folder outlining the upcoming conference in Berlin. This was strange as Yvette never made personal remarks. She was the very personification of Parisian discretion and perfect grooming as well as being the office supervisor and the arbiter of elegance. Throughout the day colleagues were forever popping into her office seeking her approval. She knew all their strengths and foibles.

"You think so? It feels good, too. Thanks." Alice rippled in response to the compliment, happy to finally be in control of her hair. Sitting with perfect posture at her meticulously ordered desk, Alice started her day with phone calls to colleagues in Asia. It was to be a day of decision and rational choices.

Meanwhile, Andy rolled out of bed, checked his vital signs and made his way to La Rotonde. Sitting at his usual table, he ordered a *tartine* and a double coffee as Manu, his usual waiter, produced the computer. Every morning Andy struggled to fit the transformer onto the cord and plug it into the stiff receptacle, but he recognized what a blessing it was not to have an Internet connection at home. Here he was at nine a.m., dressed and shaved and in the café. There was something to be said for that.

Twenty-one new emails. He opened the one from Billy first. "All's swell in Tomball. Usual ranch problems, but BP wants to exercise its right to drill the north parcel. Just thought I'd make your day. Hope you found a hair shrink for Alice."

"Waahoo! Manu, make that an Irish coffee. I've got something to celebrate!" Andy's first thought was to call Alice, but of course she wouldn't understand. Her high school teaching father and ballet dancing mother provided their only child with every luxury that Des Moines, Iowa offered. Alice had easily won a scholarship to Columbia and had married Andy a year after graduation, so she'd never had to pay an electric bill or contemplate the complexities of mortgages. His own experience had been less straightforward, but he had no intention of thinking about that right now. Right now, he wanted to hear himself talk about British Petroleum fracking on his family land.

Andy opened his phone, speed-dialed Christophe Lecerf and invited him for lunch at La Rotonde. Christophe was in executive search and hunted heads in the neighborhood so he could be counted on for lunch several times a week. He agreed to join Andy at one.

On the weekends, the Harrises had a standing invitation from the Lecerfs to join them at the Tennis Club de Paris, and Andy would order his cheeseburger there for a change. Cynthia and Christophe understood about the cheeseburgers. The Lecerfs were solid, reliable, trustworthy old friends. After Andy and Alice married they moved to Park Slope in Brooklyn where they shared a comfortable two-family brownstone and an active social life with the Lecerfs for ten years. It had been a terrible blow to the Harrises when Cynthia and Christophe returned to Paris two years ago.

Andy checked his watch. 9:30 a.m. Paris – middle of the night Stateside. The wonderful news from Billy was effervescing inside of him. It was sparkling and bubbling, becoming bigger and brighter and more encompassing. It was now seeping outside his person, filling La Rotonde and billowing out onto the Chaussée de la Muette. Soon it would be rolling down the hill to Alice's chateau-office and announce itself to her. Andy ordered a bottle of Bollinger Special Cuvee and concentrated on ESP-ing the news to Alice. He knew she'd understand how much more handsome and important and intelligent it made him, Andrew Crockett Harris, the soon-to-be rich Texas oilman. Disgraced art critic was yesterday's news. The champagne heightened the color of his glow. He was now neon-apricot.

As he leaned back in the red leather chair, a tingle spread through Andy. He recognized this tingle. He'd first experienced it with Rembrandt all those years ago. It was in the Rijksmuseum in Amsterdam he'd fallen in love with art, baffling everyone in Tomball, Texas, especially his parents and Billy. That trip had been his mother's dream, and it changed Andy's life forever.

At the time, his parents dismissed his tingle as one of his cynical jokes. But it was never a joke as his bedroom bookshelves, filled with art books, testified. Billy, on the other hand, stayed true to his ranching roots.

By the time Christophe arrived for lunch, Gregory, the manager of La Rotonde, had begun to worry about Andy. He thought of trying to reach Alice, as he knew she worked nearby but was not sure where.

"Ah, Monsieur Lecerf. Monsieur 'Arreese *est fatigué*. Maybe you'll help him home for a nap?"

"Come on, old buddy." Christophe said to Andy.

Andy looked up at Christophe. "Christo, I'm so happy."

"Me, too, Handy. Let's go."

"Stay. Have a little drink. Wanna celebrate."

"We'll celebrate at your apartment."

"Okay. Les go." Andy was slurring so badly that his friend could barely understand him.

Luckily for both of them, it was only two blocks to the Harris apartment. Christophe stood holding Andy upright in front of the entrance.

"What's the code?"

"Ah, the code. There's a 1, a 7 and an A."

"I need more than that."

"A 6. That's it. Definitely a 6."

Christophe started pushing buttons hoping for the correct combination. He knew there was a key to the apartment under the mat in the vestibule, but he had to get inside first.

Madame Barbier and Romeo opened the door. She held it wide as Christophe guided a tottering Andy into the serene marble foyer. Madame Barbier and Christophe spoke in rapid French as Andy giggled inanely and slumped against the wall. Madame Barbier and Romeo rolled their eyes, went back into their apartment and closed the door behind them.

A man doing some electrical work in the building helped Christophe get Andy up to the apartment and into bed. Christophe was sweating from the exertion and more than a little annoyed with Andy, when his friend suddenly sat up and said, "Christo, British Petroleum is dressed in white wearing a halo. It's coming to look after me and my debts." With that, he fell back into a deep sleep.

Hearing the word "debt" Christophe hesitated for a second before he called Alice. "I think Handy is 'allucinating. He's drunk and 'allucinating."

"What are you talking about, Christo? It's broad daylight. Andrew never has anything to drink in the daytime. Not since that terrible business in New York, anyway."

"Well, today must have been an exception." Christophe closed his eyes. "He said he was celebrating."

"I had a feeling that he was happy today. I had a feeling while I was on the phone to a colleague in Hong Kong that Andrew was suddenly happy, surrounded by fireworks. It was like a psychic flash."

"Don't tell anybody that you have weird ideas like this while you're at work, Alice. They're counting on you for

Rational Thought over there. And Theory-ous Decisions. Don't forget about that." Christophe and Andy had often laughed about these specialties of Alice's. "And I wouldn't tell Cynthia, either. She might haul you in for analysis." Christophe's wife was a psychiatric nurse at St. Anne's, Paris's premier psychiatric hospital.

"I don't think so. What have you done with Andrew?"

"He's in bed. I think it's safe to leave him."

"I'll be home a little after seven. I'm sure he'll be fine by then. He probably had a glass of wine with his cheeseburger without having a proper breakfast. Nothing to worry about."

"Right. Call me if you need me, anytime. You know we're always there for you guys."

Rather than wait for the elevator, Christophe chose to walk down the five flights of steps to gather his thoughts. This was not a single glass of wine, and the word "debts" disturbed him.

Patrick had told Alice to stop by anytime for a *coupe de peigne* - literally a hit of the comb, or comb-out. It is the custom in Paris to offer this as a complimentary service to good clients. Alice had finished at the office by six, and thought she'd stop by Patrick Rolland Coiffeur and have her hair put up in a chignon.

"Madame 'Arreese! What can I do?"

"Monsieur, I would love for you to put my hair up in a classic French twist."

"Avec plaisir, Madame. We will give your hair another little drink later this week. See? It likes hydration therapy."

"A little drink is always good."

"Giselle, let's all have a glass of porto. We like to have a little aperitif at this time on some days."

Alice was happy to accept the small glass. How civilized the French are, she thought, as she sipped the sweet red wine.

After adroitly arranging her hair, Patrick showed her the back of her head with a hand mirror.

"Wow. Thanks. I love it."

"Be welcome, Madame, every day."

As she was leaving, Alice took a double take. Giselle had launched into a haunting rendition of "The Way You Look Tonight". Alice had thought that Giselle spoke no English, but the lyrics were filled with such passion that she began to wonder.

Alice arrived home a little after seven. Setting down her briefcase on the marble floor and carefully hanging her coat in the hall closet, she chirped her standard greeting, "Hi, honey, I'm home."

Andy had just showered and brushed his teeth. He wore a terrycloth robe and smelled deliciously clean. First, he laughed at her joke and then said, "Hey, look at that hair. I see you went to my friend Monsieur Rolland."

"I went twice today. I love him. I love his place. All I have to do is put on a dress, and we can go on out and celebrate."

"What do you want to celebrate?" Andy was confused as he had not yet told her about the fracking.

"Whatever you want, my darling."

"Well, actually, I had some good news today. Let's get dressed and go dancing, and I'll tell you all about it."

The next morning, the electric alarm went off at seven. Neither of them was able to move, and it continued buzzing for quite some time before Andy reached over and ripped it out of the wall, silencing it forever.

"Call Yvette and tell her I'm sick, Andrew."

"I can't."

"I know."

At ten, Alice's cell rang. It was in her purse so was not too intrusive, but it was enough to wake them both.

"Call Yvette and tell her I'm sick, Andrew. Please."

Andy found his phone and made the call. "Yvette, Alice and I have food poisoning. We're both very ill. She'll be there tomorrow."

"Do you want me to call for a doctor?" Yvette asked.

"No." Andy cut the connection and went back to sleep.

Around noon, Andy brought Alice a Coke. She was pale and waxy. "Every single strand of my hair hurts. Each one is sending a separate SOS signal to my brain. My neurons are chaotic with pain. Please do something."

Andy brought three liquid Advils and the last Coke. She hadn't started drinking the first one, but he left it there, just in case.

After two of hours of silence, Alice's cell started ringing again. "I can't answer it," she whimpered.

"I know." He patted her back for a few minutes.

Around five, Andy started feeling better. "Let's go to La Rotonde. I haven't had my cheeseburger and fries."

"Okay," Alice could only agree and left the bed unmade.

On the way to the restaurant, an adult on a motorized skateboard came within a hair's breath of running into Alice. It was a close call, but Andy saved the day.

CHAPTER 3

The next day Andy spent the morning in his customary seat at La Rotonde, consulting his computer before wolfing down his cheeseburger, checking his watch and racing out the side door. He turned right and continued on to Boulevard Jules Sandeau.

Unseen by Andy, Madame Barbier and Romeo were at the other side of the intersection. Madame Barbier had lunched on a thin slice of fine Parma ham with three of her favorite cornichons and had changed into her tweed skirt with matching coat and scarf. She was looking longingly at the round tables on the pavement facing the park outside La Rotonde. She had spent many a sunny afternoon at these same tables when her finances had been different. Now such pleasures had to be limited, but she whispered to Romeo in French, "Perhaps, one sunny day in May we'll have lunch here, Romeo."

She spotted Andy and gently tugged on Romeo's leash. "I think we'll see what this Handy 'Arreese does during the day."

It was easy to spy as many people were out strolling in the spring sunshine, and she followed him at a discreet distance for several blocks, becoming increasingly agitated. Then Andy turned into an Art Nouveau building. The sinuous design on the floor was of fabulous fortune-eating vines, which pointed the way to a room on the right of the open door.

"*Mon Dieu*, Romeo," said Madame Barbier. "*Mon Dieu*." Romeo looked up at her, seeming to remember.

"Romeo, this place was the death of your father."

"Waoooo," wailed Romeo.

Madame Barbier hurried him home as fast as his stubby legs could go, all the while reminding him that *his* father – her husband – had gambled away *her* father's fortune in those very rooms. For in those very rooms were the most notorious high-stakes poker games in Paris.

Once back in her apartment, Madame Barbier consulted Romeo as to what should be done. "Should I talk to Monsieur or Madame 'Arreese about this?"

Romeo barked twice, but Madame Barbier was unsure what he meant. She went to the bureau with the secret compartment and withdrew a package carefully wrapped in a square of red silk.

Before she opened it, she secured the bolt on her door and turned on the lamp with the fringed shade. She sat on the low sofa and lit a cigarette with the heavy silver lighter, engraved with her mother's monogram. Laying the cigarette in a crystal ashtray and crossing her old, but still shapely legs, she unwrapped the tarot cards, laid them on the coffee table and smoked her cigarette with a thoughtful look on her face.

She turned over the colorful antique cards one by one, laying them in the age-old pattern. "Ooo, la, la, la, la Romeo. Come look at this." The dog scuttled to her side and drooled on the cards. "Look where the fool is and the castle. And the hangman. Something must be done."

She laid out the cards in another pattern and lit another cigarette. "What a fate! Let's see how this melds with ours." After studying the cards carefully for an hour, Madame Barbier fixed herself a cup of tea and cracked the door to the lobby. She got out her knitting and began the vigil.

A few minutes before seven, Andy was standing at the entrance. As if by magic, Madame Barbier and Romeo arrived as he succeeded in punching in the correct numbers.

"*Bonsoir*, madame. You see, I got it right this time."

"Bravo. Very impressive. Romeo and I would like to invite you to join us for coffee tomorrow morning. At nine. Would that suit your schedule?"

"As you know, madame, that is an excellent time for me." Andy looked tired, and Madame Barbier wondered what was that behind his fixed expression? Did she detect fear in his eyes?

"Very good. We'll see you in the morning."

Madame Barbier closed the door, went to her small kitchen and took down the jar of Basset hound treats. Feeding Romeo one milk bone at a time, she explained the plan to him.

"Now listen carefully. This Monsieur 'Arreese will lose all his money if he plays poker on Boulevard Jules Sandeau. He's not a bad boy, but a little immature, and we must save him."

Romeo yawned his approval.

"We'll give him our idea of the wedding chateau. He needs a job. You saw the cards." Romeo turned away from the next bone, yawned and circled around in preparation for a nap. He had heard this idea about the wedding chateau for years and was losing confidence that it would ever work out. The family chateau had been gambled away by Monsieur Barbier, and Romeo had not left Paris in over five years. He missed the country, and every time he heard the word "chateau" he missed it more. He made a morose sound and closed his bloodshot eyes.

The following morning Andy rang Madame Barbier's doorbell at nine sharp. He held out a small bouquet of roses from the nearby florist. She was flustered and touched. No one had brought her flowers for many years. Filling the precious Ming vase with water, her hand shook, and a tear slid down her pale cheek.

"Madame Barbier, please call me Andy. I'm embarrassed to have troubled you so often not remembering the code. I'm getting the hang of it now, though."

"Don't worry, Handy. Please sit down. And *merci beaucoup* for the roses. My favorite flower."

Madame Barbier smelled of Shalimar. Suddenly, Andy became alarmed that she might think of herself as a cougar and looked warily in her direction. But his apprehensions were allayed when she emerged from her kitchen staggering under the weight of a silver tray laid with an antique porcelain coffee pot, a chipped jug of hot milk and two cups and saucers, painted with roses. He could tell she was preoccupied and not interested in cougar-ing.

As she poured the strong coffee, Madame Barbier launched right in. "Handy, I hope you'll forgive me offering you advice, especially so early in the morning. I know that you Americans like to pay for advice and like it to come from a certified specialist, but here in France, it's free and comes from the heart. Please don't take offence."

"Wow, Madame Barbier, you speak perfect English. Who knew?" Andy regretted having made all the under-his-breath comments about the French.

"Don't worry, Handy. You're a fine young man, and I want to spare you some misery. So I've decided to tell you something personal. My late husband spent every afternoon on the Boulevard Jules Sandeau. It didn't work out well for him, and it won't work out well for you."

"Have you been following me?"

She raised her thin hand with the loose wedding band and lifted an eyebrow.

"I looked at the cards."

"Oh, you play poker?" Andy reached down and scratched Romeo behind his ear, wondering where this was leading.

"No, Handy. The tarot cards."

"Tarot cards? And you're worried about me?"

"I'll show you." Madame Barbier had the cards on the top of the bureau. "Come, sit on the sofa next to me so you can see for yourself."

Feeling that he should indulge her, he sat on the low Louis something-or-other sofa.

She told him to shuffle and cut the cards. Then she laid them out and explained, "You see this card? The Fool. That's you."

He leaned closer.

"You see this one? It's the castle and is good for you. You can see all the coins around the castle."

He leaned even closer.

"You see the hangman? That's poker." She moved her finger to another card. "And this card is a health problem that affects both you and Alice. What is it?"

Andy didn't answer this question. After an hour of caffeine and cards, his head was spinning.

"Voila. There it is. You talk to your wife and tell her you're going to make a good investment in a fine French chateau.

You're going to rent it out for parties and weddings. You'll make a lot of money, and Romeo and I will help you."

"Madame, I'm going to think about it. But please don't ever say anything to Alice." He got up to go but hesitated, "You know, I did have a bad day yesterday on Boulevard Jules Sandeau."

Andy left Madame Barbier's apartment and walked slower than his hunger would have wanted. He had admitted to her that the losses the previous day had been heavy, but not how heavy. He murmured twenty-three thousand euros and the amount stung the surrounding air. It was his biggest loss since being in France and had to be recouped. Madame Barbier was right. The luxurious place on the Boulevard Jules Sandeau was seductive. Someone had helped him along until he became proficient in French poker terms. And the drinks and delicious sandwiches kept him at the tables. Seductive and dangerous.

But then, he reasoned, hadn't he had a relatively good win only last week? If he took that into account, it didn't sound so bad. And he'd managed to recover bigger losses in the past. His pace quickened.

Andy went on thinking about what he had told her rather than what she had said to him. How he had been lured away from his graduate studies. *Cool Magazine* was starting up and needed someone fresh for the contemporary scene. Andy was just their man. A smart, articulate, handsome hetero hunk of a football-playing guy with a strong Texas accent who could bullshit with the best of them about art.

He was way out of the art critic mold. Really cool.

On the spur of the moment, he dropped into Patrick Rolland's.

"Ah, Monsieur 'Arreese. Be welcome. Your Madame was here, but not now. Wait 'til you see her. You must take her dancing tonight."

Andy shuddered at the prospect of more dancing as he gave himself into Giselle's hands for a shampoo.

Andy thought about one of the tarot cards, which pictured a man bent over with a load of sticks on his back. That was exactly how he felt. It reminded him of his boyhood. When he had earned a spanking, his mother would say, "You go pick your switch, Andy Harris." There he was on this card with a load of switches on his back, and he felt he deserved to be whipped with each one. All his debts were indeed a heavy load to carry.

Half-hour later, washed and blown-dry, his mood was lighter. And by the time he reached La Rotonde, dream-fracking had solved all his problems.

CHAPTER 4

By six o'clock, Andy was in a good mood. Today was a success and twenty percent of yesterday's losses had been regained on the Boulevard Jules Sandeau. "So there," he said to himself, "I wonder if the tarot cards knew that."

He finished his whisky at La Rotonde and started to think about dinner for his lovely Alice. Then he remembered Patrick's comment about going dancing. By now it wasn't such a bad idea. He hated this planning for food. Perhaps Madame Barbier was right. Perhaps he should buy a wedding chateau, hire a chef and relax a little. So far Andy had managed not to cook at home, but he was always worried his luck would run out.

For today, though, all the housekeeping he really needed to do was to get rid of the empty bottles before Alice came home. Andy appreciated the Parisian understanding of and provision for bottle disposal. Every five hundred yards in Paris there is something like a mailbox for empties. That day Andy "mailed" a week's worth of bottles. Minute after minute, bottle after bottle crashed to its symphonic death. As the dark green shards settled, a sacred silence returned. He stood there feeling exhilarated.

Andy listened to Alice's greeting and prepared himself to be cheerful. He could hear her set down the briefcase and hang her coat in the hall closet. He was smiling, but then almost fell off his throne, "Wow, Alice, those streaks!"

"Aren't they great? Even Yvette approved."

"That makes it all Parisian and fabu. Green streaks always call for a celebration, and I have the champagne already open."

"And almost empty, I see."

"It's only a little bottle. And I've got one for you."

Returning at midnight, they seeped out of the elevator onto the fifth floor landing. Getting the door unlocked was more difficult than it should have been.

Alice went straight to bed, leaving Andy in the dark living room answering his ringing phone. It was Billy.

"How's Alice's hair?"

"Slime-green. But Yvette approves."

"Are you drunk?"

"Not as drunk as I'm gonna get. Celebratin' fracking. Need an advance, though. Paris's expensive."

"Don't start counting your chickens before they hatch."

"Come on, Billy Bob, we're coming into high cotton. How 'bout we buy a chateau."

"A chateau? You are drunk, bro."

"No. Listen. There're sixteen thousand chateaux on the market, and we can get one dirt-cheap. I know someone who'll fix it up, and I'll run it for us as a fancy hotel filled with art and guests."

"Well, then, you go find one you like, and I'll crunch the numbers."

"Got to get a car for chateau shopping. Send me fifty grand?"

"Ever heard of rent-a-car?"

And the conversation drew to a close. Andy looked out of the window. On the wet street below a lone taxi was passing, windshield wipers beating violently. Uninvited an image of his ever-growing mountain of debt melded him with the darkness outside. "Poor Handy," he said aloud in the darkness.

Two mornings later, Alice set out for Patrick's. She threaded her way around the early morning dog-walking residents and children on skateboards, excited to see what the day would bring. Through the large window Alice could see him chatting and smiling as he cut someone else's hair. She felt abandoned, betrayed, usurped, and her hair needed a drink. She hesitated outside the door and then decided to come back later, at aperitif time. At that moment Lulu saw her and barked. Patrick looked up and made a move towards the door, but Alice only waved and walked on, having turned her thoughts to the more erudite questions waiting on her desk.

If she'd peered deeper into the salon, Alice would have seen her boss, Henri, with his eyes closed, being lathered by an unusually silent Giselle. Exactly when Giselle had become a permanent fixture at the salon had been lost in the annals of ever-changing hairstyles. For years Patrick's favorite aunt had often popped in, delighting the clientele with her singing. At some point, she'd seamlessly added the shampooing.

It was she who many, many years ago, sang the young Patrick to sleep while her sister continued cutting and styling late into the evening, determined to earn enough to open her own salon. Once his exhausted mother had sat down in their cluttered living room and eased her shoes off her swollen feet, Giselle would check her reflection in the mirror next to the door before heading down the five flights of stairs. Then she'd walk a mile to the jazz club where her husky voice was applauded well into the early hours.

Henri's opinions on the world and the people in it silenced Giselle, and a telling look passed between her and Patrick. They knew Henri well and much preferred his longsuffering ex-wife.

Henri's monologue continued uninterrupted as he was passed from Giselle to Patrick.

"Patrick, I recognized your signature on my sexy new colleague. The green streaks could only have come from here."

Patrick accepted the compliment with a nod of his head. Henri then spoke at length about Alice's qualities, and like a good hairdresser, Patrick listened without comment until Henri said, "I have plans for Berlin, and they don't all involve work, so make sure this cut is the best."

Patrick interrupted, something he never normally did. "And you're sure my married client is interested in you?"

"Come on, Patrick, you know me. It's the 21st century, after all. What's married got to do with it? How about a manicure?"

Knowing Henri, Patrick's brow creased in concern.

Alice had left Andy asleep. She couldn't help thinking that she'd left him in bed more mornings than not lately. We're almost back to the last few weeks in New York. This chateau idea with Madame Barbier sounds crazy, but it might be the career change he needs, she thought.

Andy didn't stay long in bed. He had plans. Apart from the little hangover, he was buoyant and full of purpose. Manu was surprised to be asked to put the computer away so soon after Andy finished his breakfast and internet browse.

Andy had meant to rent a nice sensible car, but the Hummer shining in the corner of the cramped rental lot demanded his respect for big. Its size wouldn't look amiss on the family ranch in Texas and a homesick longing for dust, heat and big sky almost brought out a tear.

Half-hour later, settling into the leather seat and running his hands around the steering wheel, his body tightening with excitement, he addressed the beige leather interior, "We don't see many like you in the sixteenth *arrondissement*. Alice and Madame Barbier will love you."

Looking down on Renaults and Peugeots and at eye level with those driving white delivery vans, Andy cruised up and down the Champs Elysées and round the Arc de Triomphe twice, to prove he could do it, before making his way to Boulevard Beauséjour. Hooted at twice for no reason, he didn't lose his temper, unlike the man on the motorbike who he really didn't see coming up on his inside.

Never having had reason to think about the width of Boulevard Beauséjour, he was struck by the narrowness of the road between the cars parked on both sides. He would have closed the wing mirrors if he only knew how, but he then quickly reminded himself that he had seen small lorries trundling past the apartment. He drove slowly, annoying those behind him. "There're always free parking spaces along here," he said. Seeing one on the right, he slowed to a crawl. "Too small." He pulled away again.

Fifty yards further on he stopped. "This one will do," and he put the Hummer in reverse. The car behind was too close and blocking the space. "Go on. Move back, buddy." Andy flapped his arm out of the window and waited while the red-faced gesticulating man in the BMW reversed. The

Hummer's loud warning bleeps made Andy jump and slam his foot on the brake. "What the hell?" He was starting to sweat. Parking in Paris is tricky, he thought and tried again, and again. "Shut up. I can do this," he shouted at the beeping, which was not quite drowning out the continuous horn blasting from the ever-extending line of cars behind him.

Whatever the words hurled at him through the Hummer window actually meant, Andy understood that the driver of the BMW was displeased. It was time to retreat with his tail between his back wheels and look elsewhere.

The five-minute drive, including two wrong turns, back to La Rotonde didn't produce any space large enough except the one designated for deliveries. He took it. Andy was an optimist, and a solution to this parking pickle was sure to arrive with his computer, cheeseburger and two small glasses of Burgundy. And sure enough, it did. His arrangement with La Rotonde now extended beyond the computer and included parking for the Hummer, at a price.

Not far away in the bar of the St. James' Club a waiter pulled the only unoccupied table half-out to allow Alice to squeeze through to the upholstered banquette behind. She apologized to the couple at the next table when her bag hit their carafe of water. The table was back in place, locking her in, and Henri Frazier, the President of Phaye, settled in opposite her. "I didn't realize this was such a popular place, perhaps we should've gone to La Rotonde."

"That's where Andy keeps his computer and eats his cheeseburger every day."

"Oh, yes, Andy. How is he? Has he learned any French?"

"A few sentences, but he makes friends easily."

"Surely not with my fellow countrymen."

"Well, our landlady wants to go into business with him, and all the waiters at La Rotonde love him."

Henri had no response to that.

As she perused the menu, Alice remembered the frown she'd seen on Yvette's usually composed face when she said she was lunching with Monsieur Frazier. She was almost sure Yvette was about to say something. Knowing Yvette was not the kind of woman to spread gossip, Alice wondered if it were about their boss.

What Alice didn't know, because at the time she was having a philosophical discussion with the head of human resources, was that Yvette had knocked on her door at noon with the intention of warning her about Henri. Getting no answer, Yvette had shrugged her shoulders and said, "She'll find out soon enough."

Henri loved his clothes and wine and labels, perhaps better than he loved his women. Like many womanizers, he knew nothing about women. Oblivious to this shortcoming, he blundered on.

After giving the waiter the order, Henri started, "So, Alice, how are you liking Paris? I'm sorry I haven't been here to show you around. I'd like to make up for that now, if you'll let me."

"I'm enjoying my work at the Institute very much...."

"Let's forget work for one lunchtime. Your hair is wonderful. The green streaks suit your eyes." He poured water into two glasses and then red wine into another two, choosing not to notice Alice's hand indicating she didn't want any. "I remember the first time I saw you. So confident, so knowledgeable. You had the audience in the palm of your hands. I knew then you were right for Phaye."

"TED preps their speakers really well. I had ten hours of personal media training for that talk."

"I'm sure you didn't need any coaching. You're a natural."

"Well, I know my subject."

Henri lifted his wine glass. Alice felt obliged to do the same. He held her eyes too long and looked too deeply. "Phaye is proud to have the world's most beautiful philosopher." Alice felt a faint repulsion as she raised her glass to her closed lips.

Henri continued seducing Alice, and Alice never noticed.

CHAPTER 5

"Hi, Honey, I'm home." It was a little after seven, and Alice had had a haircut and an aperitif. In high spirits, she was surprised and delighted to see Romeo padding towards her. Andy followed and gave her a big hug without noticing her hair. Over Andy's shoulder, Alice saw Madame Barbier rising from her "throne" holding a glass of white wine. Spread open on a couple of boxes, serving as a coffee table, were a map and several brochures.

"*Bonsoir*, Madame 'Arreese." The superb haircut was not lost on Brigitte.

Alice replied, "*Bonsoir*, Madame Barbier."

"Brigitte has found a great chateau for us to visit tomorrow," said Andy.

Alice looked pointedly at Andy as he poured a glass for her. Who was going to go without a throne? Surely not their guest, and Alice felt awkward taking what had become, through usage, Andy's.

Andy, relaxed as ever, pulled up a heavy book box for himself and triumphantly presented the brochure of the winning chateau. "We have plans to see several, but this one's our favorite, Chateau de la Vallière."

Alice looked at the moated fairytale castle. "Oh, Andrew. It's fabu! Madame Barbier, you're a wonder."

"Please call me Brigitte." She was not sure what 'fabu' meant, but Alice looked suitably dazzled.

Within minutes, she was drawn totally into Brigitte's chateau dream. "This one is perfect," extoled Brigitte. "It has towers to climb, and a maze for lovers to get lost in. So romantic and full of history. And I'm the ideal partner for Andy. He'll be the boss, and I'll run the chateau."

When the bottle was empty, Andy saw Brigitte to the door, and she said, "We should leave for the chateau by nine in the morning, but why don't you two take the rented car and explore Paris by night?"

"What a good idea." Andy called over his shoulder. "Come on, Alice. We're going touring!"

Alice was surprised when the parking valet handed over the car outside La Rotonde. "Oh, a Hummer!"

"All the better to see Paris from," he laughed. "Brigitte hasn't seen it yet."

"Let's go get the Lecerfs."

Double-parking on the rue Molitor was easy in the evening,

and Andy stayed behind the wheel while Alice dashed up to get their friends. She came down moments later with the whole family in various states of dress and undress. Squealing with delight, all four children clambered up and over into the way back. Christophe walked all around the Hummer, passing his hand over its glistening surface as he went, before getting into the front with Andy, and Cynthia slipped in next to Alice.

"You're going to have to navigate, Christo."

Christophe checked his watch. "We have eight minutes to get to the Eiffel Tower. Gun it."

"Right or left?"

"I'd better drive."

Andy and Christophe switched sides while Cynthia strapped in as many children as she could reach. And they were off.

They parked in front of the carousel across the Seine from the Eiffel Tower seconds before the light started bouncing on the Seine, passing through the open window, blessing them, drawing them into the magic. Drenching them in twinkling stars dancing from face to face.

Christophe drove around the Arc de Triomphe, and then down the Champs Elysées, around the Place de la Concorde and past the Louvre. They continued towards the Pantheon before climbing up to Montmartre to admire Paris lying at their feet. Soon regular breathing from the back signaled it was time to go home.

"Too bad we didn't have this Hummer when we drove up to Maine that summer," Christophe chuckled.

"Why we thought everyone would fit into that Buick, I don't know. Remind me how many hours we played I-spy," Andy replied.

Each adult remembered, but never said, it was always Alice having the miscarriages and Cynthia having the children.

Once back on the rue Molitor, Christophe and Cynthia struggled to get the sleepy children upstairs and back into bed. Andy took his place behind the wheel.

It wasn't long before Alice and Andy were snuggling under the goose-down duvet. Alice turned to Andy, "Our big Vipers will finally have a home. They've been in storage too long."

"Let's get the chateau first." Alice drifted off to sleep, and Andy's mind traveled back to his innocence before the fall.

It had happened so easily seven years ago in New York. Andy thought what a slick manipulator Felix Viper was. That first email to Andy - complimenting him on his reviews as being "refreshing" and "inspired", claiming that he had the rare ability to recognize innovative and emerging talent - hooked Andy in. Of course, Andy was flattered and accepted the invitation from this well-known politician. During lunch at Per Se, Congressman Viper mentioned his son, Junior. Andy had never heard of Junior, which surprised the Congressman. Andy agreed to go to Junior's studio and take a look. Even now, after all these years, he could hear the Congressman's voice, "Andy, you're going to love them.

These paintings have something special, I tell you."

Junior was out of town, and it was there in the studio that the black American Express card was produced.

Felix said, "Junior needs promotion."

Andy's thought was, "Doesn't everyone?"

Felix had gone on, "And what's the harm when someone has such great potential? Listen, Andy. A million bucks is nothing to me, but Junior can't know about the money. You enjoy this card for as long as you want. It's authorized up to $1,000,000."

In return, all Andy had to do was write favorable pieces about Junior's paintings. The Congressman would provide paintings to hang in Andy's house and office. Andy justified his actions to himself, "I was young and wanted my beautiful wife in a beautiful setting wearing beautiful clothes. We got used to going to all the smart restaurants and resorts all over the globe. I don't know how Alice thought it was possible on my expense account from *Cool*, but she never questioned it. How could I tell her the truth?" All Andy had ever wanted to do was to cover Alice with every luxury, then dig her out and start all over again.

Andy winced at how easy it had been to say "yes" and promote this young artist. Who cared? Junior did have talent. The paintings were, in fact, better than many highly priced works for sale in Soho at the time.

Junior's paintings became worth hundreds of thousands each, but Andy spent his million in four years, and his services weren't needed anymore. That couldn't have been made clearer than when he ran into Congressman Viper last year at '21'. Andy saw the adamant refusal to admit any recognition in Viper's narrowed eyes. How shiny and out-of-place the Congressman's silver-grey suit looked in that bastion of old-world elegance, and Andy wondered if Junior ever knew how it all went down.

Andy clearly remembered the very day the money ran out. The Congressman's chauffeur turned up and demanded the black American Express card. While he was at it, he removed every sign of Junior Viper from Andy's office. And once the office walls were cleared, the chauffeur insisted on going to Andy's home to collect the rest of the "Congressman's property".

Later Alice stood before the blank walls. "Andy! What happened to the Junior Vipers?"

Still grieving his loss, the truth was too difficult to tell. "I got so sick of those paintings, I sent them to storage."

"I sort of liked them and thought you did, too."

"I liked them long enough," he said.

Alice had no notion of money or any real idea how much their lifestyle cost. She knew it was beyond her assistant professor's income but never questioned Andy's expense account. Andy knew it was then that their drinking had escalated along with the debt, but no economies had been made. Everything now depended on the fracking. The sale of the mortgaged brownstone in Brooklyn would net them zero.

Andy fell into a troubled sleep.

The following morning while Andy and Alice were enjoying a long kiss in the elevator, Brigitte was having a final look at the tarot cards. "There it is again, Romeo. No mistake. The signs are good for weather and romance." Brigitte and Romeo looked at each other. "Romance. Could it be for us, Romeo?" She wrapped the cards back up in the red silk scarf, smoothed down the skirt of her full tweed outfit and, after one last check in the mirror, opened the door to join Andy and Alice. Being so very well behaved, Romeo didn't require a leash to walk up to La Rotonde.

Outside the building, Alice waved goodbye, "Have fun, you two! See you later this evening." And she headed across the Jardin du Ranelagh to the office where Yvette usually had a Nespresso selection for the thinkers.

She was literally walking across a clichéd image of springtime in Paris. The sun was starting to warm, rising sap was bursting through leaf buds, birds were singing, and she was in love with Andy and her new city. Her next thought was more practical: where could she buy a third and perhaps even a fourth chair to surprise Andy when he came home?

Out of the corner of her eye she saw two of the few people she knew in Paris standing close together. Her natural reaction would have been to join them, but she held back. It looked like they were having 'words'. Certainly neither was happy. Yvette was looking at Henri, and Henri was looking at his shoes. Before Alice had time to turn away, Yvette looked up and saw her and almost immediately so did Henri Frazier. They stopped talking, straightened, stepped back from each other and both raised an arm weakly to acknowledge Alice.

"Hi," Alice said when they were nearer, "what a wonderful morning."

"I'm late.... the metro..." offered Yvette as an explanation.

"It certainly is a wonderful morning," said Henri.

Yvette went to the right side of Alice and Henri to the left, and they walked on. A large Alsatian and small white terrier romped together in full view of a sign declaring dogs were not allowed on the grass. "You see, Alice, even our dogs ignore the rules," said Henri. Alice laughed politely and Yvette remained silent. Leaving the park, it became clear the sidewalk was too narrow to walk three abreast, forcing Yvette to reluctantly give way and fall in behind.

"I see we're both scheduled to be in Berlin the week after next for the 'Imagining the Future' conference," said Henri. "Have you been there before?"

"I've never been to Germany. So I'm really looking forward to it."

"I went to University there. I know all its hidden treasures."

"Really? This conference is going to be fascinating. My paper is called 'What went wrong? Nietzsche's Theory of Ethics'. I've almost finished it. Would you like to read it?" Alice looked at Henri earnestly.

"I'm sure it's fascinating. I'll save it for Berlin and look forward to showing you my old haunts."

Alice slowed her pace. "Do you think we'll have time? The schedule's very tight."

"We'll make time."

Alice thought she heard a snigger from behind her but couldn't be sure.

It wasn't long before they arrived at the office entrance, but it was long enough for Henri to comment favorably on Alice's hair and find out she lived close by.

Meanwhile Andy, with Brigitte and Romeo, had arrived at La Rotonde for a quick breakfast before jumping into the Hummer and heading out of Paris on their chateau hunt. Brigitte did not eat breakfast but was happy to drink a little coffee while Andy ate.

Providing breakfast and producing Andy's computer from the back room was not a problem. Producing the car was.

When Andy asked for the car to be brought round in fifteen minutes, Neil looked confused. Andy was used to people being confused by his French. Andy took a deep breath, pointed out fifteen minutes on his watch, and then pronounced *voiture* as well as he could and pointed to the street.

"But, monsieur, *pas possible* before noon." Neil shook his head while pointing to the small sandwich board outside the café, which clearly stated valet parking started at noon.

Andy thought he was pointing at an available parking spot. "I don't want to park it. I want to drive it."

"But, monsieur, I know nothing about your car. I don't even know where it is."

Andy looked to Brigitte for help, and Romeo slid under the table. After an animated conversation involving arms, many *impossibles* and as many *s'il vous plaits* during which the tension grew, Neil turned, shrugged in defeat and walked back to the office.

Brigitte finally sat down and turned to Andy. "He says it's not him. The valet parking is a separate company. He's going to try to reach them. Perhaps I will have that croissant."

It was odd how his feelings towards this woman sitting opposite had changed from distrust to trust. He sneaked a look at Brigitte as she fiddled with her croissant. Andy noticed she'd made a special effort with her hair. He was becoming quite an expert on women's hair, and he could tell she had done something different. His expertise did not extend to knowing exactly what she had done, but it was something, and he knew it. Her earrings were the same as she always wore, very fine pearl studs, and Andy always felt a special affinity with Romeo. Maybe it was the bloodshot eyes.

Taking out her cell phone, Brigitte said, "I'm just going to tell the estate agent that we'll be late."

After a conversation in French, Brigitte turned to Andy, "We'll meet the agent at the chateau at three."

To pass the time, Andy fired up his computer, and Brigitte took Romeo around the block.

Andy texted Alice. "Fly in ointment. Not seeing chateau 'til three. See you when I see you. Kisses."

CHAPTER 6

Returning from their walk a little after ten, Brigitte and Romeo couldn't help noticing a large black vehicle blocking the traffic outside La Rotonde.

"Look at that behemoth, Romeo. Who would drive a thing like that?"

Romeo gave Brigitte a dismissive look and lifted his leg.

As they came closer they saw Andy hovering near the Hummer. "*Mon Dieu*, Romeo, *mon Dieu*. I think it's ours." Romeo gave a small howl.

All the sidewalk tables outside La Rotonde were occupied by Parisians enjoying the spring sunshine. Brigitte ignored them, walked to the Hummer and stood meekly beside the passenger door.

Andy walked around from the other side. "Brigitte and Romeo, your chariot awaits."

"Romeo needs your help, Handy."

Andy was baffled by her evident lack of enthusiasm but opened the back door, and bent down low to wrap his arms around Romeo's belly, careful not to scrape his hands on the pavement. In an attempt to retain his dignity, Romeo observed silence and stiffened his whole body as he prepared to be manhandled. Unfortunately, he was placed on the floor, forcing him to spend all his available energy scrambling up onto the beige leather. The door slammed shut behind him.

"*Et moi?*" Brigitte knew this was not going to be easy. She looked down at her knee-length straight skirt.

Andy's big hands encircled her small waist as he easily lifted her onto the passenger seat. Maximizing his East Texas drawl, Andy exclaimed, "Brigitte, you such a tiny lil' ole thang!"

Brigitte broke into laughter. Real laughter. It was the first time Romeo had heard her laugh in years. His ears perked up, and he woofed with pleasure. Those seated at nearby tables clapped.

The drive to Amboise was so easy they had time to kill and, thrilled to spot a favorite restaurant from years before, Brigitte suggested they stop for a bite to eat at Le Choisel. They drove in and parked in front of the stone building. Brigitte felt more at ease by then and slipped down gracefully from the Hummer, but Romeo still needed help. As it was such a warm day, they chose to be seated in the garden and, since there was plenty of time, ordered aperitifs to mark Andy's first visit to the Loire Valley.

Andy looked worried, and Brigitte noticed his frown.

"Haven't you found anything you like?"

"To tell you the truth, I'm a cheeseburger-and-fries-guy at lunchtime."

"Perhaps you could stretch that concept a little bit."

Andy was unsure what this entailed, so Brigitte expanded. "Well, there's *steak frites*. And all the bread you could want will be in a basket. Of course, there'll be a splendid choice of cheeses afterwards. You can think of it as a deconstructed cheeseburger."

Andy pondered. If he could get some ketchup on the side, it was a stretch he was willing to make.

Brigitte turned out to be a good listener, and Andy relaxed more than he had in all the time he'd been away from New York. Before he knew it, the extent of his debts had been laid out on the starched white tablecloth between the bottle of Bollinger and the basket of homemade breads.

"I know how pride can get us into financial difficulties." Brigitte hesitated a moment and looked at the wine, ordered in honor of fracking. "I was brought up in a chateau and had a big apartment in Paris before my husband gambled it away on the Boulevard Jules Sandeau. And still after all these years, the rent you pay me has to go to pay off his debts."

"Debts," sighed Andy. "You know, when the Lecerfs left New York, Alice wanted to buy their half of the brownstone as an investment."

"That was smart thinking."

"It was the first and only time she's ever shown any interest in finances. Of course, it made perfect sense, and I felt I should honor the plan. We have a good offer on the brownstone now, but once I've paid the mortgages there'll be nothing left. I don't know how I'm going to tell Alice. She 'doesn't know from mortgages', as we say in New York."

Brigitte put her hand gently on his upper arm. "Don't say anything to Alice until we consult the cards."

Leaving the decision to the tarot cards was fine with Andy. Today it seemed like the most reasonable thing to do. Alice had the PhD in Decision Theory. And experience had produced decision phobia in him. Why not let the cards decide? Then the hangman card suddenly streaked through his mind. He didn't want Brigitte to know he'd been back to the Boulevard Jules Sandeau. He poured another glass of wine for himself. Her glass did not need topping up.

"Brigitte, do you remember you saw a health problem in the cards? Well, Alice has had three miscarriages, and the doctors say it is unlikely she can ever have a baby." Andy leaned closer. "I'd really appreciate it, if you kept that to yourself. I'm telling you because you'd be amazed how many people ask us when we're going to start a family."

"Oh, Handy, I'm so sorry."

"We have to come to terms with this, and moving to Paris is good for both of us."

After lunch backing out of the parking spot was tricky, and Andy immediately landed the Hummer in a ditch. The value of four-wheel drive became apparent, as did Andy's level of inebriation.

"Brigitte, I know deep-down you want to drive this Hummer, and I am conferring that honor on you right now," he slurred.

They switched places and, drunk as he was, Andy was able to help Brigitte make the seat petite-friendly. Seeing Brigitte at the wheel, Romeo slithered down onto the floor and put his chubby paws over his bloodshot eyes.

Brigitte's transition from passenger to driver was scary, but eventually they made it to the Chateau. The long driveway was flanked by pollarded poplar trees, which led up to a perfectly raked gravel courtyard. There pandemonium reigned.

Something was going on in the moat. Three men and two women were pointing and shouting at the water, and a basset hound was running to and fro barking joyously. One man had a rake; one man had a shovel; one man had a shotgun, and one woman wore red stilettos.

Romeo couldn't believe his big ears. He hurtled up from the floor to the height of the window in one movement to see who had this melodious voice. He only managed to glimpse a flash of tan and white hide before his breath steamed up the window. Feet scrabbling, voice vibrating and fanny wagging, Romeo demanded release.

Andy had dozed off and was a little slow to react. Brigitte turned to Romeo, "Hang on, *cheri*. I'm coming."

As soon as the back door was opened, Romeo flew out, bounced once and was gone. Brigitte staggered backwards. "Romeo, Romeo," she called.

"What's going on in that moat?" Andy asked as he pulled himself out of the car.

"They say there's a wild boar in it."

"A wild boar? In the moat? I've got to get a picture of this." Andy took out his phone as he and Brigitte walked over to join the others.

The woman in red stilettos introduced herself as the agent, Mademoiselle Dumont. She could barely be heard above all the shouting and barking.

"Get that damn pig out of the moat. I don't want to shoot it in there," said the man wearing a tweed suit and holding a shotgun.

"Get Juliette away. Where'd that other dog come from? The pig will never get out with all that yelping," shouted another man, his rake held aloft like a spear.

Andy went closer to get a better picture. Romeo and Juliette were running in tandem on the edge of the moat, excited as much by each other as by the pig. Romeo failed to swerve in time to avoid colliding with Andy, who toppled into the water.

"*Mon Dieu,* Handy, *mon dieu!*" Brigitte covered her eyes.

The man with the shotgun raised the gun to his shoulder, but being distracted by a whiff of Shalimar, lost his aim and shot in the air. The noise made the pig turn away from Andy and swim to the other side of the moat, where it clambered out. The rake was lowered, and taking hold of it, Andy scrambled up the bank.

"Mr. Harris, I presume," said the man with the gun. Romeo and Juliette were nowhere to be seen, and the others were running after the pig.

The suit lent to Andy made him look like an eighteen-year-old wearing his younger brother's clothes. Andy stood outside the open door of the paneled library where the Count, Brigitte and Mademoiselle Dumont were having tea in front of a blazing fire. He was embarrassed. He'd drunk too much. He'd ditched the Hummer. He'd fallen into the moat and was now wearing the Count's clothes. But there was no place to run. He had to face them.

Robert de la Vallière stood politely and, smiling, held his hand out to Andy and introduced himself. Andy said, "*Je suis Andy. Je suis American. Excusez-moi de ne pas parler français.*"

Robert said in perfect English, "Come and have some tea. All's well that ends well, and Romeo has met Juliette."

"And the boar? What about the wild boar?" Andy wanted to know.

"It was Juliette that hounded it into the moat. Now it's out but has run amok in the maze. In fact, it's still there, much to my gardener's chagrin."

"I see the dogs are comfortable." Romeo and Juliette were entwined in front of the fire.

Mademoiselle Dumont stood and walked over to Robert, standing a little too close, and touched his arm. "Robert, Madame Barbier and Monsieur 'Arreese must see the property before the light fades. Shall I take them around now?"

"I'll join you," Robert replied. The agent was surprised, as he had never wanted to join in on a showing before.

They started outside where it was Robert's turn to be surprised on hearing there were no orangeries in America. "Here most chateaux have orangeries since orange trees are greatly prized in France, but our climate is too harsh. For three hundred years these buildings have housed the trees in winter. We use it for many more things than orange trees now."

"What things?" Andy was curious.

"We don't have a green house, so all the delicate plants and topiaries go in, and as you can see, there's a lot of equipment stored in here. More than there should be."

Enchanted by all they saw, Andy and Brigitte followed Robert and Mademoiselle Dumont back inside and across the black and white marble entrance hall, conscious of the four centuries of feet which had crossed these same stones. Brigitte's back straightened as she walked up the center of the marble stairs, and Andy's hand caressed the sweeping rail.

With the light fading, they passed quickly from room to room and promised to come back at the weekend with Alice to show her the chateau and return the clothes. Andy and Brigitte got back in the Hummer with the reluctant Romeo. As soon as they turned onto the public road, Andy let out a whoop of laughter.

"I betcha that Ma'mzelle Dumont's steamin' now!"

"What do you mean?"

"She had her eye on that Count the whole time we were there. But he had *his* eye on you."

"Really? Do you think so?"

"I *know* so. You don't even have to look at them-there cards." Andy was exaggerating his accent again.

They both retreated into their own thoughts. Brigitte's brought a slight flush to her face, while Andy furrowed his brow. He was wondering if a chateau could ever make any money.

CHAPTER 7

Andy stood alone on the step in front of La Rotonde. He had dropped Brigitte off, the Hummer was being parked, and Alice was expecting him at home. He hesitated, and then crossed the threshold for a quiet drink to help organize his thoughts. His bank balance was not good. He ordered another drink and, leaning on the table with his chin resting in his hand, emptied his mind.

He left La Rotonde with a bag of damp clothes under his arm and waved to the staff in his enthusiastic manner, but his heart wasn't in it. For some reason the cocktails had not cheered him as they usually did. He stepped out into the misty night and crossed over to Boulevard Beauséjour. As he was going down the hill, his cell rang.

"Say, bro." The excitement in Billy's voice beaming down from the satellite made Andy feel better right away. "We've got bonus money from BP, and it's going to get the ranch out of debt."

"Out of debt?" Andy's voice was higher than normal.

"The mortgage. Remember?"

"Oh. Right." Andy cringed as he slowly remembered giving Billy his power of attorney four years ago. The medical expenses around their mother's death had eaten up what little cash was left in their father's estate, and the insurance didn't begin to cover what was necessary. How could he have forgotten?

"I'm emailing all the paperwork to you as we speak."

Andy wasn't interested in paperwork. He knew Billy was as honest as the day was long. Andy was only interested in money. "There'll be more from BP soon, won't there?" Andy stepped aside for the cyclist riding towards him on the sidewalk.

"You know we can't be sure, but my guess is we'll have something concrete by year end."

"Not 'til then?" Andy's body sagged.

"What's up? I thought you'd be pumped."

"I am, but I was just wondering about the chateau."

"Chateau? I thought that was a joke."

"Seriously, it's a good investment, and I saw the perfect one today."

"You gotta be kiddin'. You sayin' we should mortgage the *ranch* to buy a *chateau?*" Billy extended the second syllable of chateau incredulously.

Andy stopped walking and didn't speak. He wanted to go back in time and change everything. Well, not everything. Not the part about marrying Alice, of course, but Congressman Viper. And then he would have actually gone to see those shows. And no Vegas. He would have been sensible. Things would be different now.

"Andy? Andy?"

"Signal's breaking up. Call you tomorrow."

The lights in Brigitte's apartment were still on. Andy guessed the cards were keeping her busy. Passing her door, he wondered what the hangman was telling her. He didn't stop to find out. He needed Alice.

His thoughts elsewhere, Andy forgot about his attire and went straight for a hug and was perplexed when Alice took a step backwards. "What on earth do you have on?"

"What? You mean you don't like it? These are my finest chateau clothes."

Still standing in the hall after recounting the pig adventure, Andy said he needed to shower and insisted that Alice wait until Saturday to know more about the Chateau. Alice was excited about something, and once robed in terrycloth, Andy allowed himself to be led blindfolded into the living room. He smelled candles.

"Voila!" she said and held her arms out to the Lucite chairs.

"Wow. They're different."

"Yvette says they're all the rage. Louis Ghost, they're called."

"Okay, then. Fabu."

Alice nudged him into one of the stately see-though chairs and gave him a snifter of Cognac.

"Look how they reflect the candle light."

Drawing Alice onto his lap, Andy conceded that they were perfect.

"You know, it's total baloney that the French are cold and rude."

Alice told Andy she'd mentioned, in passing, that she was looking for two chairs, and Yvette had immediately suggested Louis Ghost. And Henri, who happened to pop in for something, knew just the place to get them. What was more, once Henri knew Andy wouldn't be home till late, he insisted on coming to the apartment with Alice to check the delivery, because delivery people could be difficult. Yvette agreed and said she would come too, since the apartment was on her way home.

"How lucky am I to work with such thoughtful people! It was a squeeze getting all three of us in the elevator, but we managed."

Andy stroked the clear plastic arms of what were, he had to admit, quite comfortable chairs. He thought that he should get to know Yvette and Henri.

"I opened a bottle to welcome the chairs. And they would've stayed longer if Mom hadn't phoned. I think Henri wanted to stay and have another drink, but Yvette insisted they should both go.

"Mom says they're coming to see us for their spring break. So we got the chairs just in time." Alice poured two more drinks. Andy tried and tried to imagine Herbert and Gladys Blanes in Paris. But he couldn't.

Later, as Alice dreamed peacefully, Andy's mind returned to the chateau. They hadn't managed to visit every room in the fading light, and there was a glimpse of something through a half-opened door that bothered him. He had been trying to convince himself otherwise, but even as the room grayed he could tell, there was a Viper on the far wall.

Dressed and ready to leave for the office, Alice caught sight of herself in the hall mirror. "Mirror, mirror on the wall, these green streaks won't do at all." They looked terrible in the morning light. She turned away from the mirror, put on her sunglasses and checked her watch saying, "I have time, if he does."

Through Patrick Rolland's large window Alice saw that her seat was empty. Immediately her spirits rose in expectation of Patrick's reassuring calmness, endless coffee and restorative powers.

"Please say you have time for me."

"What can I do?"

Alice recognized Romeo, lying flat out with his head on his paws, before she realized Brigitte was seated in the next chair with a black towel wrapped round her head. Romeo acknowledged Alice without enthusiasm and ignored Lulu's attempts to interest him.

"*Bonjour*, Alice. How's Handy this morning? I find Romeo is not himself. Even Lulu can't get his attention today."

Alice couldn't help watching as Brigitte's long, long tresses, customarily worn in a tight bun were revealed. From snatches of conversation between Brigitte and Giselle, Alice understood Brigitte hadn't been coloring her hair for several years. But now something had happened and Brigitte wanted to look her best. First the gray had to go, and then Patrick had to work his magic scissors on it. When her finances had been better, Brigitte had been one of Patrick's most frequent clients, and now, though they came only sporadically, she was always greeted with joy.

"Brigitte seems to know Giselle very well," Alice said, and Patrick felt he had to explain.

"They go back a long way. To late evenings in a smoke-filled piano bar. Can you imagine the atmosphere? In fact, Giselle was singing 'Blue Moon' when Monsieur Barbier proposed to Brigitte."

Brigitte turned to Alice. "You'll fall in love with the chateau, believe me. It's the kind of place where dreams come true." By the time Patrick had tempered her green streaks, Alice was convinced that Chateau de la Vallière was just the place for Andy.

Brigitte would only say "maybe" when Alice asked if she were going somewhere special. Patrick interrupted their conversation by saying, "Brigitte makes any place she goes special."

Brigitte felt light-headed when she left the salon more than an hour after Alice did. She couldn't keep her eyes away from her reflection in the shop windows. No more straight parting down the middle. No more bun on the back. Although the colorist had left some of the silvery gray, it was now streaked with dark brown. The shape was precise and modern and lifted up from her scalp. She totally approved.

"I love going to Patrick's," she sighed.

Romeo was reluctant to go for his walk and pulled on his leash. Brigitte stopped and looked down at him, "If you don't buck up, Romeo, you'll have to go to the vet." He howled and tried to move his legs faster.

At the apartment, Andy turned over, tried to go back to sleep but couldn't. It was all getting to be too much, and his face in the bathroom mirror confirmed it. He didn't believe in tarot cards but thought it wouldn't hurt to know if Brigitte had seen anything.

It wasn't long before Andy was pressing her doorbell. He did so twice, but she wasn't in. He reprimanded himself, "Come on, Andy. You can find a solution. There's always a solution."

At La Rotonde, replete with two large coffees and two *tartines*, Andy was a changed man. He opened his computer and his fingers hovered over the keyboard. "Hang it. Once an art critic...." And he plunged in typing 'Junior Viper Paris' into the search engine. The French reviews defeated him, but he didn't want to call Christophe for a translation. Christophe was bound to tell Cynthia, and she, in turn, might mention it to Alice, and he didn't want Alice to know. He kept looking.

"I know, I know, I promised to leave the art world," he said under his breath. "But I'm an ordinary American in Paris looking something up."

Andy recalled the moment he agreed to the conditions set by *Cool*. They would pay him six months' salary, and in return he was to go quietly, keep away from the art world and never write anything about what he had done, or rather not done. No one needed to know how all-consuming poker had become in his life. Even if an accusation was false, he was to keep quiet. *Cool* would handle the press, and Andy was to disappear. It was not in *Cool's* interest for the details of his wrongdoing to be generally known.

Andy closed his computer, handed it to Manu and left La Rotonde, promising to be back for lunch. It was too early for galleries to be open, but he needed some air.

Andy stamped his feet in a rare show of frustration as he read the notice in both English and French: "Mornings by appointments only." Otherwise the gallery was open from two-thirty onwards. Andy pressed his forehead against the door and peered inside at a new Viper on the left hand wall. "Damn and more damn," he said as he stepped back.

A voice called from some ways off. "Andy? Andy Harris?" He turned to see Stan Chapieski making his way towards him. Stan had gone to Columbia and the Institute of Fine Arts five years before Andy. Over the years they had developed a particular kind of camaraderie, laughing fondly about or mocking their shared professors. They were not close friends and never went out of their way to meet, although they were always happy to bump into each other at the endless openings.

Before he could say anything Stan had grabbed Andy's arm and gave him a hefty slap on the back. "Wow. It *is* you. How's it goin'?" Stan was a good five inches shorter than Andy and wore his dark hair buzzed short on the sides with the top long and held back with hidden elastic. His sharp angles and crisp clothes made Andy think of sculpture in motion. Stan was totally hip.

"It's goin'. What brings you here?" This Andy quickly realized was a stupid question to put to an art critic standing in front of an art gallery.

Unfazed, Stan nodded towards the gallery, "Same as you, man. I'm early, but if you've already finished, I'll go straight in."

Andy hadn't bothered to check if anyone was in the gallery. Stan added, "Between you and me, I've never been too keen on Viper. But you always liked him, didn't you?"

"He's okay."

"Time for a drink? I won't be in the gallery long." Stan was pointing to a café across the street. "Ten minutes max."

Andy protested that he was already running late but couldn't extract himself without exchanging cell numbers and promising to meet up. Thinking he was free, Andy was walking away when Stan called out to him again. "You know, no one gives a shit about those rumors. No one, except maybe the Congressman, that asshole."

A sharp pang went right through Andy. Was he reassured or gutted? Had he been forgiven? Not paying attention to his surroundings, he made his way back to La Rotonde and was lucky not to be run over when he walked across a side street without looking. The noises of Paris were dulled by the resurrection of memories that apparently mattered to no one but him.

True to his word, Manu had kept Andy's table free. One cheeseburger and two glasses of Burgundy later, Andy was on his way to Boulevard Jules Sandeau.

CHAPTER 8

Acting like a true Parisian, Andy double-parked the Hummer outside the apartment building on Saturday morning, blocking the entire street. Alice looked stunning as usual, but it was Brigitte who stood out. Her hair was sleek and chic. Gone were the tweeds, replaced by narrow-legged trousers hugging her slender frame and a vintage, but well-cut blazer. There was lace on her blouse, and Romeo needed only a little boost to get into the car.

Andy kept his own counsel on the way down, but this went unnoticed during the fashion discussion going on between Alice and Brigitte. Nearing Amboise, Andy pointed out that they were going to be early. His suggestion of parking nearby was turned down. Brigitte preferred a walk around the grounds if they couldn't tour the chateau right away, and Alice agreed.

"Oh, Andrew, it's *fabu*," said Alice on her first sight of Chateau de la Vallière gleaming in the spring sunshine. The Count and Mademoiselle Dumont were standing together at the end of the driveway, deep in conversation, beside the calm moat. Romeo made such a din that Brigitte had to let him out before Andy could turn off the engine. Juliette's whole body wagged in welcome.

Robert de la Vallière strode towards them. He went straight to Brigitte with his arms outstretched and, holding on to both her hands, said quite a lot before turning to Alice and Andy. He said, "I'm so sorry I have been called away on urgent business. But I'm leaving you in the capable hands of Mademoiselle Dumont."

Standing behind Robert, Mademoiselle Dumont was beaming. Brigitte was not. But it was only seconds before she mustered a halfhearted smile, though disappointment tarried in her eyes.

Robert apologized again as he got into his old gray Peugeot, "You may decide against the property, but please come back as my guests for lunch next Sunday."

Brigitte lingered, watching Robert drive off, as the others followed Mademoiselle Dumont into the chateau.

Once inside Andy excused himself while Mademoiselle Dumont gave a well-rehearsed lecture on the chateau's place in history. She began, "This was the childhood home of Louise de la Vallière, Louis XIV's first mistress and mother of four of his children."

Andy was not interested in Louise. He wanted to locate the Viper in hopes of keeping Alice away from it. "Up and left, or is it right?" he asked himself. Turning left, he recognized the polished wooden floor with the worn red patterned carpet running its length. But something was wrong. "No, this isn't right." He went back to the stairs and took the corridor going the opposite way. "This is it. Walls with good portraits and very fine 17ᵗʰ century chairs." He bent to touch their fabric before he sped on. How he missed the art world! Paintings were his first love and furniture came a close second.

There were voices nearby. He hadn't reckoned on others being in the chateau. There were two of them, one male, one female, just round the next corner. In panic Andy pushed open the nearest door and fell into a massive bathroom from another era. Straight ahead was the original, discolored porcelain bath, and on another wall a matching pedestal basin with old-fashioned taps. And then his heart stopped. Not one but two distinctive Vipers were demanding his attention on the wall next to the door he'd just closed. The voices outside passed unawares.

Even from a distance Andy felt an affinity for these paintings. He went closer. "Oh my God," he said, "these are really good." He remembered catching sight of what were probably similar works, stacked up in a corner of Viper's studio years ago. Junior had called it his practice pile and had not wanted Andy to look at them. Now on close inspection, however, Andy was excited by the raw power of the work and the unexpected vibrancy of color. "This is Junior at his best," Andy said out loud.

A second door in the bathroom led to a bedroom, where Andy found the Viper he'd seen from a distance. It, too, was a very early one. And superb. Andy felt a chill go up his spine as his cell rang. "Andrew, where are you? Are you all right?"

"On my way." And he cut the connection. He took a long look at the painting on the bedroom wall, sighed and left the room.

Andy saw some stairs up ahead and seconds later was rushing down into the cellars of the chateau. "Where's the front of this place?" he pleaded aloud. Then he heard more voices, or were they the same? Andy swerved into the nearest room, pushing open a very solid wooden door. Suddenly, he was face to face with a large skinless animal dangling from a hook in the ceiling.

"*Zut alors.*" The voice came from the boar.

Andy staggered back against the door. A head peeked around the carcass. "Ah, Mr. America. From the moat. *Voila*, monsieur, your pig."

Andy recognized him, even without a rake. "Please help me. I'm lost."

"Ah, we're all lost, monsieur," the man said philosophically.

Andy could tell that meant problems, long winded problems.

"No. No. No. I'm really lost." Andy was impatient.

Andy's cell rang making both men jump.

"Andrew? What *are* you doing?"

"Just a bit lost." And before he could stop himself, he said, "Start without me, darlin'."

"Ok. You find us."

Andy groaned loudly and slid down the wall onto his haunches. He so didn't want Alice to see the Vipers. He could just imagine it. Alice would declare Andy as the expert and was sure to say they had some in storage, which they didn't.

The man tapped the side of his nose with his index finger, put down a large knife and said, "Follow me, monsieur".

But it was too late. Alice was in the bedroom, telling Brigitte and Mademoiselle Dumont about Andy's expertise with respect to Junior.

"In a farce", Andy said to himself, "this is where I'd collapse." Listening, he waited for the right moment to appear. To his horror, both Mademoiselle Dumont and Brigitte were fascinated and asked many questions, which Alice answered to the full extent of her knowledge. Enough was enough.

"Hello, ladies. Sorry I took so long, but this is one big chateau." He grinned.

As soon as he could, Andy took Alice aside. "As you know, darlin', I'm always in favor of honesty, but you've got to find that place between the truth and the whole truth and stay there."

"Where's that, Andrew?"

Andy looked at her as if to say, 'You've *got* to be kidding.'

"You know, discretion." He said, "You have to be discreet."

"But Brigitte and Mademoiselle Dumont are our *friends.*"

"No, Alice. We don't even know our real estate agent's first name and Brigitte - as much as I like her - is our landlady, whom we've only known for three months." Brigitte overheard this exchange and nodded in agreement. She was proud of Andy. She thought of him as "her" Andy. He was maturing. It would take some time, but he was maturing. And Alice, well, Alice might take a bit longer.

Andy wanted to be alone with the Vipers, but Mademoiselle Dumont moved them along leading them from one room to another. Suddenly, they were at the top of a staircase that Andy recognized. "I went down those stairs just after I heard voices up here. Who else lives in the chateau?"

Mademoiselle Dumont straightened her spine. "The Count lives here alone. He's a widower. His son is a jazz musician in New York, and his daughter is a lawyer in Paris."

Alice asked, "Why is he selling?" At the same time Andy asked, "Whose voices did I hear?"

Mademoiselle Dumont looked straight at Andy. "I can't imagine. The Count said the chateau was empty, apart from the cook and gardener."

"Well, for sure I saw the gardener downstairs with the pig, but who was upstairs?"

Mademoiselle Dumont pursed her lips and shrugged her shoulders. "Didn't I mention the ghosts, monsieur?"

Until now Brigitte had kept her distance from Mademoiselle Dumont, but this was too fascinating. "Are they 18th century ghosts?"

"I have not met them personally, but others claim a young couple and their parrot from the Napoleonic era haunt the chateau. So not 18th century, but early 19th."

"Why aren't they resting in peace?" Brigitte wanted to know.

Mademoiselle Dumont tried to close the subject by opening another door. "From here there's a wonderful view of the gardens. I shouldn't have said anything. Anyway, this gossip is two hundred years old. Let's move on, shall we?"

"Americans don't believe in ghosts," said Alice. "It's irrational."

"How can you say that? Most of my best friends are ghosts," said Brigitte.

"You're kidding. But, really, why is he selling his ancestral chateau?"

"The chateau is too big, and he's looking for a manor house nearby."

"Wow. Look at that." They all joined Andy peering out of a window overlooking the maze. "What a mess that pig made," he said.

"*Mon Dieu*. Those hedges must be fifty years old. They'll never grow back in the Count's lifetime," Brigitte said sadly.

Andy, like most Texans, knew all about wild pigs and was more than happy to share his knowledge on the subject. He ended by saying, "That's why we need to eat them. And the one hanging downstairs will soon be ready to go into the oven."

Everyone was quiet on the drive back to Paris. It wasn't until they were almost home that Alice said, "Oh, I forgot, my parents arrive next Sunday. Do you think they can come to the chateau for lunch, too? My mother would die to meet a real Count."

Brigitte was jolted alert and accidently bumped Romeo's head. Romeo growled in his sleep, and Andy said, "You know, they'll be jet-lagged, darlin'. They arrive at six. They'll want to recover, never having been to Europe and all. First-time jet lag is the worst."

"I know, Andrew, but they would love the chateau and the Count. Nobody in Des Moines has ever had lunch with a Count in his chateau."

"It's a real shame they can't come, but they'll be too tired."

"You're right."

As soon as they got back to the apartment, Alice closed the door to the bedroom behind her and called her mother. "Mom, you've got to change the plane tickets and come a couple of days earlier. On Sunday, we're invited by Count de la Vallière for lunch at his chateau. It was built in the 1650s."

"Oh, my God! We wouldn't miss *that* for the *world*!"

"Oh, Mom, you're going to love it." Alice thought how wonderful it would be. "Andy's thinking of buying it as an investment. A place for weddings, corporate retreats and so forth."

"Built in the 1650s! What will Andy think of next? Good thing we're already packed. I'll just add something special to wear to the chateau. Don't you worry your pretty little head, Sugarfoot. We'll be there by Thursday or Friday at the latest with bells on."

"I'm so excited! Tell Daddy I love him. And email me the flight change."

Alice went into the living room where Andy was reading the *International New York Times* with great interest. It was Chapieski's review of the Viper show.

"Guess what, Andrew?"

Not looking up from the paper, Andy made a guessing sound.

"My parents are changing their flight and will be well rested in time for lunch on Sunday. I'm going downstairs right now to ask Brigitte to see if that's okay. It would *make* their trip."

Andy slowly lowered the newspaper. His face had gone pale. His eyes were blank. He could well imagine the Blanes at the Chateau. "No," he said. "I'll go ask her."

Andy took the steps two at a time and had his hand raised to tap on Brigitte's door when he heard the singing. It was a full-throated rendition of 'La Vie en Rose'. Andy stood in the hall transfixed. She came to the end, but Andy couldn't wait any longer and knocked loudly.

"Oh, Handy!" Brigitte was all smiles and Shalimar.

"Sorry to butt in like this, but Alice's parents are coming earlier than expected, and she wants to see if they can come to lunch on Sunday."

Brigitte's expression was a bit stiff as she opened the door for Andy.

"Could we take a look at the cards?" Andy asked.

Brigitte was quick to get them. Andy shuffled and cut them into three piles, as instructed. Looking intently at the cards laid before her, Brigitte began, "I see you've been back to the Boulevard Jules Sandeau. I see you've been back more than once, and I'm very disappointed. You see where the hangman is?"

The hangman was front and center with the man with the sticks on his back right on top. Andy could not take his eyes away from the cards to face Brigitte. Accusation and guilt jarred the air between them.

Brigitte returned to the cards, "I see lots of money trying to come to you, but this hangman is not good for you. You see this card?" Brigitte pointed. "There's a man, blond or gray haired, who is your enemy in the work domain. This man is powerful and does not like you. Do you know who I mean?"

"Maybe." Andy knew it was the Congressman.

"And here is a dark-haired man bringing you news about him."

"What does it say about that?"

"It's not clear. It's murky. Has to do with the distant past and the recent past. And look - here are two intruders. Be sure you lock all your doors and windows."

"Maybe they're Alice's parents," Andy said as he readjusted himself on the low sofa. Andy liked Alice's parents; he liked their kindness, their intelligence, their loyalty, but the truth was they embarrassed him. It was the way they dressed, what they said, even their display of affection for each other and Alice. Herbert talked with his mouth full and called Alice "Sugar-baby", and Gladys called her "Sugarfoot". Andy couldn't stand it and hated himself for being so superficial, but there it was. He could cope in Des Moines, but anywhere else they were intruders in his life with Alice. She adored her parents and seemed totally oblivious to this. But he sensed that Gladys and Herb knew how he felt. And the worst part of it all was, they loved him anyway. Andy looked at the card with the man bent over with sticks on his back. "Portrait of Handy", he thought.

"Shuffle again. Cut into two and give me half." Brigitte broke into his reverie.

"Oh, this is beautiful. There's love and money everywhere. Look, Handy."

Andy looked but didn't see anything.

"I've read the cards for forty years, and I've never seen anything as beautiful as this. Now give me the other half."

Her tone changed. "You're at a crossroad. You must be very careful. A great deal is at stake. Did you notice all the love and money was in one pile, and all the danger was in the other? You can have disaster and sickness or love and wealth. Shuffle and give me fifteen cards."

Brigitte laid the cards out slowly and then sat for a moment contemplating them. "The crossroad. Come see me before you make any major decisions. Keep your secrets to yourself, and don't go anywhere near the Boulevard Jules Sandeau, Handy. Everything could work out for your benefit, or you could throw it all away. Is there anything you want to ask?"

Andy had many questions fighting for his attention, but he said "No. Thank you, Brigitte. I'll call you if I think of anything."

He took the stairs, realizing that he needed some exercise. Even though it was dark, he was going for a jog. The first one since arriving in Paris. As he pounded the pavement of Paris, the image of the hangman haunted him. He could feel the noose tightening around his own neck. And he couldn't tell Alice about why he left *Cool* or why their finances were in such a perilous state because he would have to admit to gambling and that he hadn't told the whole truth. No point in alarming her, after all. Of course, his luck will come back and with it all the money lost at the poker table. What would be the sense in worrying her about things, which will shortly be sorted out?

An hour later, sweaty in his tracksuit, Andy paused outside Brigitte's door. He had an urgent question, but her lights were out.

CHAPTER 9

Andy arranged to meet Stan for coffee at a café near his favorite Shakespeare and Co. bookshop with the intention of spending some time browsing beforehand, but his heart wasn't in it. It was raining and cold. Andy left the bookshop and went to the café, chose a table facing the door and ordered a double coffee.

Andy saw Stan come in and waved. "Hey. What'll it be?"

"Just coffee for me. Thanks."

Andy ordered two coffees, and they traded the usual pleasantries. "That was a good review you wrote."

"Thanks. What are you up to now?"

"I'm taking a long break from the art world. Alice got this amazing offer from a think tank here in Paris, and I'm just trailing behind and contemplating changing careers."

"Changing careers? Do you seriously think there's any other world for people like us?"

"I'm ready for something new. Maybe a special event chateau or even a vineyard."

"You can't just quit the art world."

"I can. Total abstinence. I haven't been inside one gallery since I arrived in Paris. The closest I got was when you saw me the other day."

Andy told a few funny stories about his recent life, and neither he nor Stan mentioned his sudden departure from New York again. Andy wasn't sure whether this was because his brief explanation was all that was needed or if Stan just wasn't interested.

Their conversation became stilted, and Andy left it to Stan to delve into deeper waters.

"I meant what I said about the gossip, Andy. What are we meant to be doing as art critics? Scrutinize? Analyze? Explain what the artist means? Between you and me, sometimes I have no bloody idea what it means. And on top of that, we're meant to say whether it's any good. We know it's all subjective, yet we're supposed to be clear and objective."

"Yeah," Andy agreed. "The bullshit level's really cranking up."

"Know what you mean. I decided to stop reading comments on my articles, but then, I was told by my editor if I didn't, I'd be out on my ass. When I pointed out we didn't respond to comment before all this blogging and tweeting, I was accused of being reactionary and told to 'embrace' progress. What a load of crap. Mind you, if I responded to all of the negative shit, I'd go mad."

Andy couldn't hold back any longer, "The other day you mentioned Congressman Viper."

"Oh yeah. Outside that gallery. You know, I've been to so many places and talked to so many people in the last few days…. meant to be at another *vernissage* at this precise moment, but I can't be bothered. I'll look at other reviews and write it up. I'll take it from the French ones. Lucky I can speak the lingo."

Andy was getting annoyed, and his face showed it.

Stan got it. "Oh, right. That was one of the things going round about you, wasn't it? And the other nonsense. Didn't you read it?"

"Read what? What other nonsense?"

"That piece. Where Viper senior went out of his way to put you down? Where he claimed you'd taken one of Junior's early works? Then up popped Junior defending you, saying he'd offered you a whole pile of early works, and you didn't take a single one. Junior claimed you said it was unethical, so that shut the Congressman up. Everyone was surprised you didn't respond. Junior probably ditched all that early work in one of his tantrums anyway. He never let anyone near it. And who doesn't have freebies, for God's sake? I'll bet the Congressman's pile is enormous. Want to come with me to this exhibition?"

Andy was surprised that he regretted having to decline Stan's invitation, and he was surprised about Junior's having defended him. And he wondered if he really would have refused Junior's offer to take the paintings. Anyway, it had never happened. So why had he claimed it? Junior had always kept a drop cloth over that stack. Andy had only glimpsed the paintings, and he'd never actually *owned* a Viper.

Stan laughed, "If we went to all those openings and drank all that champagne and ate all those hors d'oeuvres, we'd be drunks the size of busses."

It was good that Stan talked so much. It gave Andy time to compose himself, bring himself back to the present. Stan leaned over to get his iPad out of his shoulder bag and started what he really wanted to say. "As you're taking a break from it all, Andy, you couldn't run your eyes over a few pieces for me, could you? You know so much more than I do about contemporary stuff." Andy was happy to listen, read and comment. It was easier than thinking, and he didn't mind sharing his opinion.

It wasn't long before Andy retreated to the comfort of La Rotonde. Christophe Lecerf was passing by, saw Andy and came to join him.

"Andy! So glad you're here. Today is Cynthia's birthday. Come shopping with me. I never know what to get."

"Christo, you've come to the expert in such matters. Your solution is just around the corner: a gift certificate from Patrick Rolland, the coiffeur. Every woman loves him. Have a glass of wine and then let's go."

Just as they were about to leave, Andy's cell rang. It was Alice. "Andrew, it's Cynthia's birthday. I almost forgot because I'm so excited that Mom and Dad are coming."

"Everything's under control. Christo's here and we're going to have dinner – the four of us – tonight. And Cynthia's going to get hair time with Patrick for her birthday."

"Great idea. She'll love him. If you're heading that way, please make an appointment for me at six-thirty. I need a tune-up if we're going out tonight."

Christophe and Andy walked from the noisy street into the calm. "Patrick, my friend here wants a gift certificate for his wife, I want my usual, and Alice wants to come in to see you at six-thirty."

"Can do. My pleasure."

"There you are, Christophe. Problem solved. You can thank me with a fine wine later." Andy turned to leave, but his friend decided to stay.

Patrick had a strict rule that he never interfered with a client's business. He never passed on gossip and never tried to change the course of events. That wasn't his job. Clients sought his advice, and he supported their views. But today he was sorely tempted. He had a soft spot for Andy, who was definitely not up to speed on cultural differences, especially French wooing techniques. Scissors in hand, Patrick cleared his throat, "Monsieur Lecerf, your American friends are very nice."

"Yes," Christophe yawned and picked up a back issue of Gala.

Patrick wanted to say that Andy needed to be warned that Henri was after Alice. He wanted to discuss Americans and mention that they should not be so trusting. He wanted to explain the traditional *cinq à sept*. Five to seven p.m. being the traditional extramarital affaire hours in France. But he simply could not break his strict rule and continued cutting Christophe's hair with a loud soliloquy thrashing around his head.

In the end, Christophe turned right on Avenue Mozart and headed home, none the wiser.

Alice hadn't been totally truthful when she'd cited too much work as her reason for not joining Henri for lunch, and to make it look legitimate, she felt compelled to eat a sandwich at her desk. Alice was making a list. A list of all the places Andy could show her parents while she was at the office. She wanted them to have the best time so they'd agree to come back and spend the whole summer in France.

Yvette tapped lightly on her open door before placing a folder on Alice's desk. "Voilà, all the final bits for Berlin. Does Andy like the chairs?"

"He certainly does, and so will my parents. You're just the person to tell me what they should really see in Paris, Yvette."

Yvette promised to come up with ideas and started for the door, but turned back. "Will you still want to go to Berlin while they're here? We could cancel."

"It's only a couple of nights. They get on so well with Andrew, it's not a problem."

"So you will go to Berlin, then?"

Alice tapped the folder Yvette had just placed before her, "Everything's written and set, and Henri has already made arrangements to show me an interesting part of Berlin."

Yvette looked at Alice. "It's unlike him to be so organized."

"Then it's good he's organized this time so we all know what we're doing."

"Do we?" said Yvette in a slightly higher tone than normal as she turned and went on her way.

"Really must do something about getting those two together," thought Alice as she went back to her list.

But her thoughts drifted to Henri and Yvette. She knew he was too shy to ask the sensational Yvette out. He was lonely. Why else was he always popping round to their side of the building to ask Alice simple questions if it wasn't to be near Yvette? She had met men before who found a married woman easier to talk to than the actual object of their desire. Alice considered the situation carefully from all sides. She was a skilled matchmaker. She would ask them over for drinks to get them started before her parents arrived.

All four children were sitting around the dining room table in the Lecerf's apartment, eating birthday cake when Andy and Alice arrived. The last time Cynthia had seen Alice was in the Hummer when it was dark, and she hadn't noticed the startling green streaks in Alice's hair. Cynthia's eyebrows shot up, and she sucked in her breath, "They really are bright, your streaks, Alice."

"Do you like them?"

"I do, but does Andy? Here, take a seat. Have some cake."

"He thinks they're fabu. You can get some, too. This is delicious."

Cynthia laughed, "I don't think Christophe would like me with green streaks."

"He may be right. You'd look better with pink ones."

"Pink ones?"

"Yes, bright pink ones in your brunette hair would look wonderful. Don't you think so, Christo?" Christophe and Andy were in deep conversation at the other end of the table.

"Don't forget Cynthia works at a psychiatric hospital, Alice. I don't want her to be confused with her patients."

"Christo, you're so rude," laughed Alice.

Christophe quickly responded, "Rude to whom?"

"To me and the patients and Patrick Rolland, of course. Did I tell you my precious parents are arriving the day after tomorrow?"

"Oh, so nice! Have them join us at the TCP on Saturday." Cynthia and Christophe had met the Blanes in New York several times. Cynthia found and appreciated their good qualities.

"Great idea," said Alice to Cynthia. "They love to play tennis. Maybe they could borrow some rackets and play with Christophe and Andy. We could be the cheerleaders." And so it was settled that there would be a tennis match on Saturday morning at ten.

All four children admired Alice's hair, and by the time they were all in bed, Cynthia had been persuaded to try at least one narrow pink streak behind one ear.

Cynthia was looking forward to having a few moments alone with Alice and took the opportunity when Andy and Christophe turned on the television.

"How's the sale of the brownstone coming along?" Cynthia asked.

"I leave all that to Andy. He's in charge of our finances."

"Is that wise?"

"Wiser that having me in charge. Give me a theory to dissect, and I'm as happy as a clam at high tide, but put me with the finances, and I'm totally useless. You know that."

"I'd always want to make sure all the "i"s are dotted and the "t"s are crossed.

CHAPTER 10

Before leaving for work the next day, Alice nudged Andy to check if he were awake and reminded him, "I've invited Yvette and Henri over for drinks after work today." Andy grunted as she set out her plan. "I think they'd be perfect together. I mean really together, not just colleagues. So can you please get some romantic food and drink?"

Vaguely wondering what romantic food and drink were and hating this part of trailing, Andy made an affirmative sound, turned over and went back to sleep.

After his lunch, Andy wandered into the wine shop and arranged for a case of Prosecco rosé to be delivered. He then went to the nearby cheese shop. He pointed to a heart-shaped one, muttering, "How romantic is that?" And then asked the mature lady behind the counter to choose a dozen kinds for him. This was confusing for him and her, but finally he left with twelve different cheeses, numbered as to the order in which they should be eaten. So the French even have a proper order in which to eat cheese, Andy thought as he trudged up the five flights of stairs, burdened by two hefty bags. Walking up was now part of his fitness regime.

"Oh, God," he said when he got to the top. "I forgot to tell them at La Rotonde I need the car at five in the morning." Andy was trapped waiting for the wine delivery. He tried to call them, but the language barrier was too challenging. He would have to go there once the wine was in the fridge. But the cheese was taking up all the available room. He started talking to himself, "Okay. Leave the cheese out. Prosecco rosé *has* to be cold. This fridge is only *so* big. Get used to the smell of cheese."

He left the apartment with the wine deliveryman. They took the elevator down in silence, and Andy walked through the Jardin du Ranelagh to La Rotonde. He was going to have to park the Hummer himself. The very thought of this was too much. Andy dragged his feet. When he got to La Rotonde he ordered a martini. He'd not had one in a long time. He asked for extra olives and sat at the bar chatting with Kaya, the barman. No, he didn't want his computer, but he would love the valet parker to find a spot from where the Hummer could be extracted at five in the morning.

The parker was a most accommodating person, and offered to put the Hummer in a garage open twenty-four hours a little farther away, but still in the neighborhood.

That sounded great to Andy, and he ordered another martini while he waited for the valet to return with the car keys.

The pungent odor of cheese smacked Alice as she got off the elevator. "Hi, honey. I'm home." She walked straight into the living room and threw open all three windows, despite the chilliness of the day. Then she went to the kitchen, and she shrieked when she saw the amount of cheese. She knew Andy had done his best, and so as he came into the kitchen, she gave him a big hug and said, "It's *so* romantic to have such a lovely selection of cheese."

"Your hair looks beautiful, and so do you."

"Look, I've brought gorgeous grapes. And what are we drinking?" Alice unwrapped the grapes, put them in a colander in the sink and turned on the tap.

"Prosecco rosé."

"What fun! Let's have a glass before they get here." The doorbell rang at that very moment.

It was Henri with a huge bouquet of flowers. Alice couldn't find a vase large enough and put them in a red plastic bucket, which she placed on a box in the living room. Henri didn't comment on the quantity of cheese, but Alice did notice his eyes and nostrils widen.

Alas, there were no breads or crackers to go with the cheese, but there were plenty of grapes, and the fridge was full to capacity with twelve bottles of Prosecco rosé, eight bottles of various white wines, three bottles of French rosé and four magnums of champagne. There was half a jar of Dijon mustard and a full bottle of capers. Again, Henri didn't comment. Alice thought of her parents arriving in the morning and worried they would be startled that there was no milk or Coke or butter or eggs or yogurt or anything that was in their own fridge in Des Moines. However, there *were* two pints of Häagen-Dazs chocolate in the freezer, which she'd gotten especially for her mother.

"Oh, Andrew, we forgot the bread."

Andy knew that meant *he* forgot the bread. This was another of his jobs. Picking up his keys, he murmured, "Back in five minutes."

Andy's leaving suited Henri to a tee. He sauntered into the living room and sat on Andy's throne, holding a glass of Prosecco in one hand and a hunk of blue cheese in the other. "This is such a nice place, Alice. I'm glad our agent found something within walking distance of the office. Easy to pop home to during the day. We like our philosophers to be happy."

Alice only had time to say, "We love it here," before Henri leaned over and pulled the other throne close to his and suggested Alice sit next to him. He then picked up the bottle to top up their glasses.

Henri was very interested in the apartment and whether Andy was in or out all day.

Meanwhile Andy was hurrying back from the bakery with three baguettes tucked under his arm when he recognized the person walking in front of him.

"*Bonsoir*, Yvette. I know where you're going; let me escort you."

Yvette turned and laughed. Once inside the elevator Yvette asked Andy if he knew Henri well. Andy said, "No, we've only met a few times." Yvette looked into his eyes and said, "He has quite a reputation with the ladies." She tilted her head to one side, thinking Andy understood. Andy didn't get any message.

Alice was fussing in the kitchen when Andy and Yvette came through the door. Yvette handed Alice a cream-colored box tied with a yellow ribbon, which Alice recognized as coming from the expensive chocolate shop around the corner. Alice thought the chocolates would make a nice addition to her parents' food supply, and took it from Yvette with unbecoming quickness. She then darted into the guest bedroom and placed it on the bedside box.

"Yvette, what will you have, Prosecco rosé or champagne?" Alice put her hand gently on her colleague's shoulder to guide her. "Come and sit down in the living room next to Henri, and Andy and I will bring in the wine and cheese."

"I'll have champagne. *Merci*, Alice." Yvette sat in one of the ghost chairs opposite Henri. Silent and moody, they sat waiting for the Harrises to come back. Henri stood as Alice came into the room carrying a glass for Yvette and one for herself. Andy followed with the ironing board. It was draped in a plastic bag and covered with cheese and grapes. "It's a buffet," he said as he set it up near an open window.

It got chillier as the evening went on, and Alice passed out sweaters and shawls rather than close the windows on the smelly cheese. It seemed that neither Yvette nor Henri wanted the evening to end. Andy thought he caught a whiff of combativeness between the two of them, and around midnight he tiptoed into the bedroom, set the alarm for four-thirty and collapsed.

No one seemed to notice he was gone until finally Henri looked at his watch and remembered that Alice's parents were due to arrive. "I'm so sorry, *ma chérie*. We have over-stayed our welcome, but you are such a charming hostess and your cheeses are so extraordinary, I couldn't tear myself away. And, Yvette, I know you have an early day tomorrow so we must leave Alice, but first we'll help you with the glasses."

Two were broken during the washing up, and finally the guests departed. In all there were eight empty wine bottles. Alice put them in a bag to tidy up the kitchen and put that bag under the bed. Sound asleep, Andy snored through the clanking. She left the ironing board set up by the window, covering it with several dishcloths, hoping her parents wouldn't notice the smell. Then she, too, fell into bed.

Soon the alarm was exploding next to her ear. Alice shot out of bed. Her first thought was how happy she was that her parents were arriving. This happiness was somewhat dampened by a headache and the strong odor of cheese. Andy was up and brushing his teeth as Alice got dressed. She stuffed as much of the cheese as possible into the refrigerator. She couldn't do anything about the rest, and she left the ironing board where it was. They raced down the stairs to find the car and get to the airport. Alice wanted to be the first sight her parents saw coming out of customs.

"Where's the car, Andrew?"

"In the garage down the street. I've got all the details written down." Andy pulled out his wallet as they half-walked, half-ran. "I know I put the piece of paper in here." Andy pulled out scrap after scrap with 11A77 written in Brigitte's clear handwriting. When they arrived at the garage, Andy was still searching.

"What floor, Andrew?"

"Where the fuck is it?" Andy pulled everything out of his wallet. Receipts, notes, more bits of paper fell to the floor. He checked again but it wasn't there.

"Damn it, Andrew!"

"It'll be easy to spot. Good thing it's a Hummer."

Now they were running from level to level. Andy held the

key ring high above his head, pressing the 'open' button again and again, but no car lights blinked in recognition. They rushed down and down.

"How could anyone lose something so big?" Alice was crying.

"There it is!" screamed Andy. He scrambled into the driver's seat, but it was too tight for Alice to get in on the other side. Andy started the engine and pulled forward. Alice climbed in before he noticed the size of the car parked opposite. The Hummer's warning beeps got louder and louder. There wasn't space for him to turn.

"Damn and more damn! Don't you bleep at me. Don't you know I have eyes? That's it, I'm changing you for a Smart. Alice, please get out and help me."

"My parents won't fit into a Smart."

"Just get out and tell me how close I am."

He went backwards and forwards time and again, inching the Hummer around. Andy rationalized that he'd barely touched the cars around him, and anyway, most cars in Paris were full of dents. He hoped no one checked the cameras.

The Hummer arrived at the exit barrier, but where was the ticket to get out?

CHAPTER 11

Herb and Gladys's flight arrived bang on time. Alice's was the first face they saw. Gladys was wearing ill-fitting denim jeans and jacket with a red, white and black plaid flannel shirt, tucked in, white socks and impressive black and red athletic shoes. Herb wore black jogging pants with matching hoodie, a plain white tee shirt and sneakers that matched Gladys's. Herb's hair was still dark brown, like his bright eyes, but thinning. Gladys's was shoulder length - salt and pepper.

Andy had been very careful about where he parked the Hummer at the airport, so once the luggage was loaded, they were on their way. Laughter and chatter filled the car through the morning rush hour back into Paris. It continued as they walked up the stairs, since the luggage took over the entire elevator. Andy was impressed that Herb and Gladys kept up the pace while talking a blue streak.

On seeing the apartment, Gladys exclaimed, "Oh, kids, this is magnificent! Look at the ceilings and the floors, and oh, these moldings, Herb. It's like a mini-mansion, isn't it? I just can't believe I'm really here." Neither one of them mentioned the smell of cheese nor the unusual cheese board.

"I'll help you settle in, Mom."

"And, Sugarfoot, I just can't get over how much I love your darling green streaks. Herb, don't you just love Alice's darling green streaks?"

"Now, don't you go getting any big ideas, Glady. They're darling on Alice, but I like your hair just like it is." He gave his wife and daughter a long group hug. Andy had had enough and went to check on the cheese.

"Oh, Mom and Dad, I'm *so* happy you're here!"

Although tired, her parents were persuaded to have breakfast at La Rotonde from where Alice went off to the office. They were still wearing their traveling clothes.

"Another coffee?" asked Andy.

"Sure and how about another round of those *tartines*?" Herb raised his arm high and waved it around saying, "*Garçon, garçon.*" He had a voice that carried.

Andy reached over and pressed Herb's arm down. "Let me order. It's good practice for me."

"Aw, come on, Andy, I've never gotten to speak French to French people, and I studied it for years."

"Boys, boys. We can all speak as much French as we want in Paris. But could we get whatever either of you would like to go? I'm wilting fast."

Herb looked concerned and reached over and patted Gladys's hand. "I don't need anything. Let's get my princess to her bed. Paris is a long way from Des Moines."

Back on the Boulevard Beauséjour, Andy explained how to get into the apartment building and was giving them each a slip of paper pulled from his wallet, with the code clearly written on it. When Brigitte and Romeo came out of their apartment, Andy did the introductions.

"Madame and Monsieur Blanes, you are so welcome to Paris. I look forward to our lunch in the country on Sunday." Andy recognized the little twinkle in her eye.

"And we're so happy to meet *you*, Madame Brigitte and this fine Romeo of yours. I just love that you called us 'Madame' and 'Monsieur'! And I just can't believe we're going to meet a real live Count complete with ancestral chateau! Aren't we the *luckiest*? I'm sure we'll have a real, real good time."

To Andy and Brigitte's astonishment, Gladys then lifted her leg gracefully and pressed the elevator button with her foot in full point. She went up in the elevator with Herb while Andy ran up the stairs.

Gladys and Herb flopped onto their bed and were asleep in minutes. Andy also needed some peace and went back down the stairs and across the road into the Jardin du Ranelagh.

Andy chose an empty bench in the shade rather than share one in the sun. Although squeals and shouts from the children's playground overlaid the traffic noise, it was peaceful. But he was not happy. Being accused of stealing by Congressman Viper was bugging him. He was guilty of a number of things, but not that. True, he'd cut himself adrift from the art world, but in a way that was a challenge he wanted to know if he could meet. If he hadn't met Stan Chapieski by chance, he never would have known.

His cell rang; it was Stan.

"How you doin'?" Andy asked.

"Great. I wanted to thank you for your insights the other day. Have you read any of my reviews?"

"Not yet."

"You must. *They* all got good reviews themselves. Words like 'pertinent', 'insightful', 'refreshing'. We're doing reviews of reviews now. What a load of crap."

"Critics criticizing criticism – it could go on and on." As he said that Andy had an idea, but Stan had one too.

"How about coming to a *vernissage* with me this evening? The subject is right up your alley. Or, if you can't make it, do you have time for a quick coffee this afternoon? I'd like to run something by you," Stan said.

Andy was set on poker that afternoon, despite Brigitte's plea. His chances to go to Boulevard Jules Sandeau would be few and far between for the next two weeks, and a plan was forming in Andy's mind and Stan was in it. What was the harm in going as someone's guest to an opening? It wasn't as if he would write anything.

"I'm supposed to be 'in-law sitting', but I know Alice would love some time alone with her parents." They arranged to meet at Les Deux Magots just before six.

Andy put the phone in his pocket and leaned back on the bench. He mumbled, "You scratch my back, Stan buddy, and I'll scratch yours." And then, whistling softly he said to himself, "Get a load of this!" He spied not only Brigitte and Romeo but also Robert de la Vallière and Juliette walking into the park. They hadn't seen him, and he wasn't going to spoil their time together. He hummed as he walked in the opposite direction taking the long route to the Boulevard Jules Sandeau.

CHAPTER 12

Gladys woke before Herb, and for a moment didn't know where she was. The window and the door were in the wrong place, and the outside noises were odd, as was the smell. Then data started uploading. The familiar snore to her left meant she was safe, and a nanosecond later she remembered she was in Paris. She lay there and let herself feel the thrill. A big smile spread over her face.

Herb stirred but didn't wake as Gladys tiptoed back and forth between the bedroom and bathroom getting dressed. Through the windows, the sights were just like those in the tourist guide in her suitcase. Narrower streets filled with smaller cars and slate roofs crowning fine architecture. She stood at the window and soaked it all in.

Knowing Herb would want a snack when he woke, Gladys moved on to the kitchen and opened the fridge. Her eyes widened. Packages of cheese were stuffed in, over and around three bottles of Prosecco rosé, eight bottles of various white wines, three bottles of French rosé, three magnums of champagne, half a jar of Dijon mustard and a full bottle of capers. She searched the kitchen and was surprised to find nothing familiar. No coffee or tea, no sugar or flour, no salt or pepper, no Fruit Loops or Captain Crunch. She followed her nose to the living room. Under the tea towels on the ironing board, she found stale baguettes and even more cheese.

Gladys went back to the kitchen and opened the freezer on the off chance that all the missing edibles would be crowded in there. She cried out in delight when she saw the familiar packaging of her favorite ice cream. "Oh, and it's chocolate," she sighed. Not finding any bowls, she helped herself to the carton and two spoons and went back to awaken Herb. Herb was not interested in waking up, so she returned to the window and ate the whole pint looking out over the trees.

Fully caffeinated and sugared-up, she went in search of the Hoover. First she did the living room and hall, and then moved on to the master bedroom, where she clanked into the black plastic bag from the night before. She pulled it out and looked inside. Nine empty Prosecco bottles and one empty magnum of champagne. "What a funny place to keep the recycling," she thought.

"Glady-honey." She heard the plaintive cry and came to the door of the guest bedroom. "I'm hungry. Any chance of a cup of tea and some toast?"

"How about some wine and cheese? I can bring you that, and there's a box of chocolates on that box by your head. We can picnic right here on the bed."

"I just woke up, honey-pie. I definitely don't want any wine or cheese or chocolate. Just toast with butter and jam and a nice cup of tea."

Gladys raised her arms to fifth position, pirouetted and said, "This is Paris, Herby. I'm coming with the wine and cheese. No fussing."

She sprinkled the stale baguette with water, popped it in the oven and covered it with a tea towel while she sniffed around and found the three mildest cheeses and opened a bottle of French rosé. Before she had a chance to arrange all this on the one and only tray, Herb was standing behind her wearing only his boxer shorts.

"You're going to catch your death of cold wandering around this apartment in your skivvies. I'm so glad the kids like fresh air, but it's too cold. Now, you go dress while I bring this into the dining room."

The dining room had yet to be used by the Harrises. They had other priorities. There was a large table left by a previous tenant, but no chairs, so it had to be the ghosts or the thrones. Gladys opted for the ghosts. She brought the red plastic bucket of flowers and placed them in the middle of the table. Dressed in his blue plaid flannel shirt and no-nonsense jeans, Herb joined her a few moments later.

"Glady-honey, I just *can't* drink wine right now. Can't I just have a Coke or a glass of milk?"

"Now, Herby, we're guests here in Alice's household. Remember how different it was at their apartment in Brooklyn from our house in Des Moines?"

"Yes." Herb paused and thought back on how different it was.

"Well, Paris is even more different. In Paris they don't bother with food. It's just wine and cheese and restaurants. That's what it's going to be for two weeks. And we're going to love it."

"Can't we go to the grocery?"

"How would *you* feel if Alice and Andy came to *our* house and looked around *our* kitchen, then rushed right out to the grocery?"

"I would feel just fine, wouldn't you?"

"No, I would *not.* I would feel like I wasn't a good hostess. And we would *never* want our *darling* Alice to think we thought that about *her.*"

"You know, Glady-girl, I love you all day long every day, but sometimes I think you're flat-out crazy. What on Earth is wrong with providing for ourselves?"

"Just hush, Herby, and be happy."

Herb took a sip of wine and made a face. "Are we allowed to go to that restaurant up the road?"

"We're going to stay right here and make ourselves useful until one of them comes home. Then we'll see."

"All righty, then. What do you want me to do?"

"Well, the recycling is under the kids' bed. Why don't you take that down to Madame Brigitte and ask her where it goes? It must have been collecting there for weeks. There're ten wine bottles, and one of them is really big."

"You don't think they're drinking too much, do you?"

"Heavens, no. This is Paris. The wine here is better for you than the water. Everyone knows that. What time is it?"

"Six-fifty-two p.m., local time; eleven-fifty-two a.m., Des Moines." Just then the phone mounted on the kitchen wall started ringing. Herb went to answer it.

"That's fine, just fine. Your mother will want to know what she should wear." And a few seconds later. "Love you, too."

"What?"

"Alice says Andy has to meet a colleague, but she'll be here in a few minutes, and we're going to a cozy little place for dinner. Doesn't matter what you wear."

"Doesn't matter what I *wear*? We're in Paris, Herby. Of course it matters. I'm going to change." She posed in arabesque and vanished into the bedroom.

Andy left his poker game, got on the metro and arrived before Stan at Les Deux Magots. Sitting there alone, he envisioned a group of surrealists led by Salvador Dali arguing loudly in the corner, and Hemingway ordering another drink from the table next to his. Jean-Paul Sartre and Simone de Beauvoir had their heads together, philosophizing no doubt. It was a place of intrigue and passion where dreams and reality could mix, and he was planning a little foray himself.

Stan didn't look well as he sat down opposite, but Andy was too polite to say anything. "The gallery isn't far away. Finish your drink and we'll push off." A few minutes later Stan launched into his work problems, saying he was blocked. Andy's request to spread a few words on his behalf to several New York art critics seemed paltry in comparison.

"Consider it done, Andy. Everyone knows Congressman Viper's claim was totally bogus and malicious. Especially since you had always promoted Junior."

Andy was well aware that he had promoted Junior, and also that he'd been well paid for it. He knew the Congressman would keep their guilty little secret, but Andy wasn't going to let the Congressman tar him with theft. He may not have attended every single show he reviewed, but he was not a thief.

The *vernissage* was in a small gallery, and the atmosphere was like a homecoming, with smells of canvas, paint and champagne. And wonder of wonders, this artist had talent. Andy stood alone, taking in every piece.

Stan came up behind him, beads of sweat forming on his brow. "I'm bewildered by it. I don't know anymore whether it's good, crap or nondescript."

"Forget the hype on the handout and don't listen to anyone else. Take it from me, this is very, very good. And it has nothing to do with what's in the brochure. Write what I tell you and promote her for the right reasons before others do."

By the time Andy left the gallery, he had missed most of dinner with Alice and her parents. But he didn't mind, and they would forgive him. He was on a high and mused as he swayed on the metro. What were the odds of bumping into Stan? He couldn't calculate them. It was an awesome break.

The next morning Herb woke before the others. He knew he couldn't face wine and cheese for breakfast and sneaked out of the apartment in search of real food.

An hour later, propping the bags of essentials against the wall outside the entrance door, Herb congratulated himself on his use of French and finding his way back. He pulled out the keys for the inner door and felt for the scrap of paper with the code. He tried all his pockets but it wasn't there. It was on the bedside box. Contentment turned to despair. He could remember a couple of numbers, but that was all.

He pressed a combination of buttons. Nothing happened. Another combination and then another.

He looked up. There was no point in shouting; the apartment faced the other side.

Shrugging in resignation, Herb slumped down on the doorstep to wait until someone came. He leaned back against the door, but he kept going and going until he was flat on his back almost looking up Brigitte's skirt. Romeo snuffled his ear.

"You've forgotten ze code, Monsieur Blanes. I write it for you." Brigitte held out a piece of paper.

Red in the face, Herb jumped to his feet, took the paper, thanked Brigitte and wished her a good day.

"I think you have forgotten something, Monsieur Blanes. Perhaps it's ze jet-lag." Smiling, she handed him first one bag and then another.

"I'd invite you to breakfast, but they only have four chairs."

It was no surprise to Herb to find Gladys at the kitchen sink washing last night's glasses. Two empty magnums of champagne were on the counter waiting to be recycled.

"Look what I've got!" Herb opened a bag filled with every kind of croissant for Gladys's inspection.

"Hush, Herby-honey, they're still sleeping, and I can't find a kettle, but water's boiling in that skillet. Oh, so smart. You bought mugs and bowls."

"In case there aren't enough here. And, look, *pain au chocolat.*"

They emptied the bags, squeezing around each other opening the fridge and cupboards that were, until then, bare.

"Glady, did you notice how much they drank last night?" whispered Herb.

"It was to celebrate our arrival. That champagne went right to my head. They're so happy we're here. Where shall we sit?"

"Well, the chairs are in the living room."

Half-hour later, Alice emerged from the bedroom. "Oh! You two look like the king and queen bee, sitting on those thrones."

Behind them the ironing board was spread with a wealth of croissants, butter, jam, a saucepan of tea and one of coffee, a vase of milk and four kinds of cereal. Gladys raised her tea in the new mug in welcome. Herb raised his bowl in similar fashion.

"Come on in and join us, Sugar-baby," Herb bellowed, cornflakes flying.

"I know why the Lecerfs came back to Paris. They missed their morning goodies too much. With all these yummies, how do they stay so thin?" Herb said gesturing to Alice to serve herself. "I ate three before the cornflakes."

"They're thin because they don't eat three. And they came back for the children to have a French education."

"What's wrong with a good old American education? They could've moved to Des Moines if they wanted a first rate one."

Alice feared a long discourse on the pros and cons of education coming on and made her excuses to leave. Gladys was more direct. "Stop it, Herby. Stop it right now. And have another croissant."

CHAPTER 13

The time had come to outfit the Blanes with tennis attire. Fortunately the Tennis Club de Paris no longer required whites, but Gladys was taller than Alice, and Herb was shorter than Andy. Everything was too short for Gladys and too long for Herb, but they didn't seem to mind. They had on their matching red and black sneakers and were anxious to get going.

Christophe was waiting for them and introduced them to the TCP pro, who looked askance at Alice's parents. As he handed over two ratty loaner racquets, he said, "Monsieur Lecerf, there has been a change of court. You will be on court twenty today." This was a hard court with a backboard for children to practice on. Christophe had reserved a clay court and thought what a snob the pro was, but decided not to comment.

The Parisians noticed Gladys and Herb as they walked to the far away court. Embarrassed Andy kept his eyes on the path ahead. He had warned Christophe not to expect a good game. Gladys taught ballet, and Herb, English Literature, as well as coaching the baseball team at Roosevelt High School in Des Moines, but as far as Andy knew they were as proficient as they looked.

"Would you like to warm up for a few minutes, Gladys?" Christophe was so polite.

"No thanks, Christo-honey. Herb and I are good to go. We walked over here. But we haven't played since last summer, so don't expect too much."

Andy and Christophe caught each other's eyes as they took their positions awaiting Gladys's serve. It came at such a speed that Andy didn't even swing. Andy and Christophe didn't score in the first set, not even when Christophe was serving. He had a well-respected serve, and today he didn't hold back.

Someone had mentioned to the pro that there was quite a game going on court twenty. He paid no attention, but his assistant went out to watch the second set. Both Andy and Christophe were sweating hard, but the Blanes were cool and chatted loudly between themselves as if they were home alone back in Iowa. Andy got through this by pretending to himself they were Christophe's parents-in-law.

"How about playing the best of five?" Herb shouted over the net as he and Gladys took the second set.

With their honor at stake and people beginning to watch, they agreed. "They must tire soon, mustn't they?" muttered a weary Christophe.

Andy and Christophe squeaked out a win in set three, and there was quite a crowd around court twenty when they started the fourth. As this was an out-of-the-way court, there was no seating, but people were peering over each other's shoulders trying to get the best view.

"What was that about not expecting a good game?" huffed Christophe. He, too, was becoming embarrassed as the number of observers increased. He and Andy were collecting balls from their end of the court again.

The club champion went into the pro shop and demanded to know why this game was not on court one. "Monsieur Lecerf told me his guests were not regular players, monsieur. I'm so sorry."

"I'd like to play with this couple, if you can arrange it."

By the time Cynthia, with a hot pink streak behind her left ear, and Alice, with renewed green ones, arrived, the Blanes were on court one, holding their own with the club champions even after whipping Andy and Christophe. The last set was a struggle for all four, but in the end Herb and Gladys won, two – one. The whole gallery burst into applause, and Gladys didn't hesitate to make a full Swan Lake-type curtsey, a big smile spread all over her face. The Parisians totally loved it.

Meanwhile back on Boulevard Beauséjour, Brigitte was baffled and concerned by the cards. "Romeo, this could all go very wrong. We have to speak to Handy before tomorrow. I'll leave the door ajar, and you tell me when he comes in."

Romeo took up his position by the door.

Gladys and Herb were bundles of energy, but Andy was beat. He was happy to help Alice and her parents find a taxi for their trip to the Louvre, but he was looking forward to collapsing in bed for the afternoon.

Romeo gave a little woof as Andy pushed the entrance door open, and Brigitte appeared at her door to ask him in. Andy sensed urgency in her invitation and without a word followed her wearily as if he were being led to the principal's office.

"What's this I see in the cards? What are you doing on the wrong path?"

Andy looked at Romeo for support but Romeo's big eyes reproached him, too. Brigitte motioned him to sit down. There was an uneasy silence until Brigitte said, "I don't need to show you the cards. We both know. Not only are you still gambling, you're heading for conflict with a very powerful blond or gray-haired man. You're playing with fire. What's wrong with you?"

This time Andy did respond. "I can't just sit back and be maligned like that. The man you see in the cards publicly inferred that I am a thief. I can't let him get away with it. I had to do something when the opportunity was staring me in the face."

"And the gambling?"

"That's simple. I need a big win."

Andy saw a change in Brigitte's manner as he told her he'd lost heavily the previous day and the sale of the brownstone was about to go through. Alice still believed there would be a pot of money. He hadn't been able to tell her about the mortgages. Or that he did not actually own any Vipers. Plus Billy had no more news from BP. There might well be money, maybe even lots of it, eventually. But at this moment he was desperate.

Brigitte stared straight into his eyes, "You have to tell Alice. You don't have a choice."

"I can't. I can't burst her bubble while her parents are here. Alice is so close to them and this would be another secret she would have to keep. The miscarriages and not being able to have children are enough. Besides Herb and Gladys would never understand about the money."

Brigitte reached out to stroke his arm, but Andy pulled back and changed the subject.

"So what did the cards say about Romeo? Will he succumb to Juliette?" Andy arched his eyebrow playfully.

Brigitte took Andy's lead, "Something about old dogs and new tricks comes to mind."

"And what about Brigitte and the Count? I saw you two the other day. I doubt he came all the way to Paris to take Juliette shopping."

Andy was sure Brigitte blushed as a smile lit her face. "Robert and I are *not* old dogs, and as for new tricks..."

"Ah ha, it's Robert now, is it? And what should I call him tomorrow?"

"Just introduce him as Robert de la Vallière. It's for him to tell you to call him Robert. That's how we do it here. And now you should go. Tomorrow I'll tell you about the ghosts in the chateau: Mathilde, Olivier and Captain, the parrot."

"Oh, come on, Brigitte, you don't really believe in ghosts, do you?"

"It's no more irrational to believe in them than not to."

Andy let that pass, but as he was leaving, he paused, "I love the art world. I hate being cut off from it. Will you look at the cards and see if there's a way back in?"

"Of course, I will. See you in the morning."

That night it was wine and cheese in moderation *chez* Harris and early to bed.

Sun streamed into the building on Boulevard Beauséjour that Sunday morning. The fifth and ground floors were jumping with preparations. Hair dryers, magnifying mirrors, tweezers, brushes, bath salts, make-up and perfume were being used with abandon.

Gladys slipped on her calf-length green chiffon dress with woven-in sparkles and tied her hair back with a green velvet ribbon. Just as she was taking her matching green satin ballet slippers out of the tissue paper, Alice knocked perfunctorily and walked in wearing a cream-colored linen Armani pants suit.

"How fabu are you, Mom? And look how great we go together! Your dress and my hair!"

"I know, Sugarfoot! I was so excited when I saw your streaks! The exact same green. I knew we would be poetry together. We'll ask Daddy what the poem is. He'll know."

Alice and Gladys hugged each other and beamed. Herb came in dressed in his special occasion dark gray pinstriped suit with a Hawaiian motif tie. He brightened when he saw his girls. "Oh, my stars! Andy and I are the two luckiest ducks to be going to lunch with the prettiest girls in Paris."

"I just love how Mom and I match! And, Daddy, you *are* the luckiest duck to be married to Mom!"

Herb said, "The way a team plays as a whole determines its success."

"Your favorite baseball philosopher, right Dad? Babe Ruth?"

Gladys then slipped on a pair of glasses.

"Since when have you needed glasses, Mom?"

"Since never, but these are like jewelry. I got them at Haynes' Antique store. They're mother-of-pearl."

"I say she is the mother of a real pearl!" They group hugged.

Andy came to the door in a blue blazer over a white polo shirt and khakis. His smile stayed fixed. He really hated himself for being embarrassed by the Blanes. At least Alice was always chic.

"I'm going to get the Hummer. I'll call Alice's cell when I get close. Then, could you go get Brigitte and Romeo and meet me out front?" He would run to the garage to blow off steam.

While Alice locked the door, Gladys pirouetted and called the elevator with her perfectly pointed green satin toe. Her big smile set the tone for the day.

CHAPTER 14

Excitement in the middle row of the Hummer fizzed up and overflowed on first sight of the Chateau.

"Look at that! Where's my camera? People back home won't believe it." Herb scrambled in his backpack.

Gladys whooped. "Those turrets! It's like Disneyland."

Alice, in the middle seat, grabbed a hand of each parent, "Mom, Dad, you'll so love living in one of those towers."

Brigitte, seated up front with Andy, turned and looked at him, but he steadfastly kept his eyes on the chateau's long drive.

"Wow, there's a moat, with water in it. Where's the drawbridge? There's bound to be a drawbridge."

Andy mumbled to himself something about probably not getting a cheeseburger for lunch but fortunately, no one heard him. He couldn't even hear himself.

"You *sure* are wearing the right dress. Come on, Cinderella, we're going to the *ball*." Herb reached over Alice and grabbed Gladys's hand.

"Is that the Count, Sugarfoot? Who's that with him?" Gladys asked.

"Well, it's not Mademoiselle Dumont," said Andy as he turned the engine off.

Romeo escaped as soon as Brigitte opened her door and made a beeline for Juliette.

"That hound knows a good thing when he sees it." Herb clambered out and started to follow Brigitte, who was making her way towards Robert de la Vallière.

Robert kissed Brigitte on both cheeks and presented his daughter, Sophie.

Being the perfect gentleman, Robert kissed Alice's hand. Gladys' eyes misted over when the Count bowed and took her hand to his lips. She flourished into the lowest curtsey possible and remained there for some time, while reaching up to keep a tight grip on Robert's hand.

The ground beneath Andy did not open up, and Brigitte maintained her perfect posture. Greetings between the men were less challenging. Herb clasped the Count's hand firmly and congratulated him on having a great place.

Once everyone was settled on the terrace, Robert brought Sophie to meet Andy. He'd understood from Brigitte that Andy was a famous art critic and an expert on Viper. He couldn't have been more surprised that anyone had ever heard of this artist, much less be an expert on him. The paintings belonged to Sophie and were not at all to his taste, but he listened to them chat about Junior for a while before making his excuses and moving on to look after his other guests.

Right away Sophie said, "I recognize your name. Don't you do contemporary art for *Cool*?"

"Not since I've moved to Paris."

"Are you working here now?"

Andy hesitated. "I'm taking some time out."

"So what are you doing?"

Andy's first thoughts were playing poker and consulting the Tarot cards, but he said, "I'm researching some ideas."

Sophie took the hint and let the matter drop.

A combination of Sophie's charm and Robert's champagne eased Andy's tension, and he started to relax for the first time that day. He listened to Sophie recall her year at Yale University where she and Junior had been undergraduates together. She described him as a stunningly good-looking longhaired boy with dark brown eyes who knew masses about philosophy and art, but who was moody and somewhat of a loner. They became friends - nothing serious - and he had given her these three paintings, which he'd figured were the best he'd done up to that point. She had always liked them as they reminded her of her year in the States, and she'd kept them wherever she lived all through University and Law school. She now lived in Paris and had just recently retired the paintings to her childhood bedroom and bath. She'd been delighted to read Stan Chapieski's recent review of the Viper show in Paris and was eager to hear more. Andy had to admit he hadn't yet seen the show.

Sophie invited Andy to her bedroom, "to see her paintings, of course." Champagne in hand, they stood before the Vipers, and Andy found himself itching to write about them, thinking this "practice period" might be the most important in Junior's career. They were gutsy. Much more exciting than the later, more polished work. He was also interested to hear that Sophie had met the Congressman and had noticed the tension between father and son. She said Junior was adamant he would make it on his own and resented his father coming up with schemes to push his work.

Sophie glanced down at her watch. "We have to join the others for lunch or Pierre and Marie Jo will have a fit. They have been with Papa for nearly thirty years and, believe me, we live by their rules. They'll be as relieved as Papa when you buy the Chateau. My brother, Jacques, has moved to New York, so it's lonely here for just the three of them. And I'm sure you and Alice will be very happy here." Andy thought about his impecunious state, felt a zing of panic and managed to smile.

They arrived on the terrace just in time. When English-speaking guests were at the Chateau, Pierre liked to say in perfect British butler fashion, "Luncheon is served, my Lord."

Gladys was thrilled to be seated on Robert's right. "Oh, my goodness. There must be a whole bush of lilacs on this table, and look at those peonies. Lord Count, this is the most beautiful dining room I've ever seen."

"Thank you, Mrs. Blanes. Please call me Robert. And I would like to call you Gladys, if I may."

"Gracious, yes, Robert. Herb calls me Glady, but you can call me anything you want. And I know a lot about furniture since Andy has all those books, and I can tell this mahogany table dates from the reign of Napoleon, as do the chairs. And the sculptures in the niches represent Spring and Summer."

"You are one hundred percent correct, isn't she, *chérie*?" Robert turned to Sophie, who was seated between Brigitte and Andy.

"Indeed she is, Papa. And you have said just the right thing as Papa is fiercely proud of this table. It's seventy-two inches in diameter - one solid piece of mahogany. It was made especially for this room, commissioned for one of our ancestors."

"Oh, my lands, imagine that! And look at the ceiling all painted to look like the sky. And a checkerboard marble floor, too. This is just what a chateau should look like, don't you think so, Herby?"

"I don't really know what a chateau should look like, Glady, but Robert sure has a nice spread here."

After the watercress soup, the pig arrived with an apple in its mouth. It accompanied a savory apple crumble, shredded

Brussels sprouts tossed in butter and tiny new potatoes seasoned with nutmeg.

"Do you recognize your friend, Andy?" Robert gestured to the platter. "He's swimming in sparkling cider this time."

The conversation for the rest of the meal was devoted to describing to Sophie and the Blanes what happened in the moat and the maze. Andy made a few protests while secretly enjoying the good-humored teasing. It was decided that after strawberries and cream, Alice would show the Chateau to her parents, and Andy and Sophie would photograph the Vipers. Robert and Brigitte would meet them in the drawing room with coffee.

Squeals of delight echoed in and out of rooms, up and down the hallways as Alice led her parents around the Chateau, and Gladys pronounced first this room and then the next one was the most magnificent.

"Pinch me, Sugarfoot." Gladys said to Alice.

"You girls were born for castles," said Herb, "and this one fits you like a glove."

In front of one bedroom window, Gladys held both of Alice's hands in hers, "I can't make up my mind about which bedroom is best, but for sure I can hear the pitter-patter of tiny feet. You and Andy are going to have to have a passel of kids to fill this place." Herb agreed enthusiastically.

Gladys and Herb would never hurt Alice, but hurt her they had, to her very core.

Caught off-guard, Alice said, "I'm just going to leave you for a couple of minutes. Go on ahead. I'll find you."

Once out of sight, Alice breathed deeply as the physical pain receded. It wouldn't take her long to recover, and even though she was used to hearing such comments, the hurt was fresh each time. Not today, but one day, she would have to tell her parents there would never be any grandchildren.

Herb and Gladys took a narrow wooden staircase up to the attic. The room was large and neglected with a few scattered bits of furniture from different epochs.

Gladys ran her hand over a broken rocking horse. "Maybe you can repair this, Herby. It can be your first job here. Wouldn't it be great for the grandkids?"

They didn't notice the refined young couple standing in the far corner of the room. The young lady came up behind the Blanes as they looked out of a round window and spoke softly into Gladys's ear.

"The Count says the attic has the best view. It's possible to see for miles."

Gladys's ballet training helped her as she spun around without losing her balance, "What the heck?" She paused and looked at the young couple, dressed in Napoleonic attire. "Oh, look at you two, all dressed up! You gave me such a fright. We almost jumped right out of our skins, didn't we, Herby."

"We sure did. Hi, I'm Herbert Blanes, and this is my wife, Gladys. The Count said we could look all over the Chateau."

Olivier bowed to them. Gladys lowered herself into another extended curtsey, and Herb nodded and extended his hand.

"We are Olivier and Mathilde de la Vallière. Our naughty parrot, Captain, is in the garden." Olivier didn't seem to notice Herb's outstretched hand.

"You should have joined us for lunch. It was delicious." Herb offered.

Mathilde turned to Gladys, "Do you think I should wear the sapphire or diamond pendant? Olivier gave me both today, but he refuses to say which he prefers."

"The blue definitely. It matches your eyes. Have you ever thought of blue streaks for your hair? It's all the rage. Listen, we're going for a walk in the garden. Why don't you two join us?"

"I regret we cannot. We must be going, Mathilde. Everyone will be waiting to say goodbye. The carriage is at the door," Olivier said.

"See you downstairs, then." Gladys gave them her wide smile and a little wave.

In the blue drawing room, Robert and Brigitte were delighted to be alone at last. This was just the kind of room Brigitte knew as a child. It was formally and classically French. The pale blue paneling and floors were original to the chateau, making them mid-17th century, but all the furniture, paintings, mirrors, porcelains and Aubusson carpet were Louis XV, mid-18th century. Two small Salvador Dali sculptures, a few ashtrays and lamps were the only representatives of the modern era. The silks on the furniture were woven in Lyon, as were the curtains. The room had looked much the same for hundreds of years. Robert's ancestor who had commissioned the dining room table would have recognized it as his own.

They were just settling in on the sofa when the dogs started making a terrible racket. On the other side of the moat, Romeo and Juliette were baying at an orange tree. Robert and Brigitte crossed the bridge to investigate.

Brigitte couldn't believe her ears. It sounded like the topiary was barking. "It's the ghost of that damn parrot," Robert said. "He's been teasing the dogs of this house for two hundred years. He loves to wind Juliette up like this and then lead her on a merry chase. No harm, really. She enjoys him."

"Captain!" called Brigitte firmly. She knew how to talk to parrots.

"Captain, Captain, Captain," was the reply from the tree.

"You're a noisy boy today."

"Shut up. Shut up. Shut up, Captain," squawked the tree.

"Can you see him in there? I've never seen a ghost," Brigitte sighed.

"Neither have I, but I certainly hear from this one a lot."

"I found out about Mathilde and Olivier from one of our mutual friends."

"We have mutual friends, do we? How convenient." Robert smiled at Brigitte.

"Such a tragic story. Leaving for their honeymoon and everyone killed in that carriage accident. I gathered the ghosts of the coachman and the horses are heard roaring around the countryside in the fall."

"I've never heard them, but Captain barks and whistles and moos and mews and whinnies and oinks and quacks and trumpets and roars at the darnedest times. It's like being in an invisible zoo indoors and out."

"You mean you've lived here your whole life and you've never seen Mathilde and Olivier?"

"I don't think anyone's seen them since my grandfather's time."

"Andy heard them last weekend."

"Oh, really? We hear them occasionally, and they say, it's good luck. I wish you would stay here with me and my ghosts."

Just then Sophie called from the window, "Alice can't find her parents. Keep an eye out for them, Papa."

"Look around for them inside, darling, and Brigitte and I will search the garden." Robert put his hand on the small of Brigitte's back and steered her toward the rose garden.

Half an hour later, and they'd all returned to the blue room. "We ran into Olivier and Mathilde trying on fancy clothes in the attic." All eyes went to Gladys.

"Oh?" Robert tried to sound nonchalant.

"Herby told them what a delicious lunch they'd missed, and they said they'd be down later. Those kids look a little pale, Robert. I told them they should come for a walk with us in the garden, you know, get some fresh air. I thought they liked the idea, but they just sort of disappeared. I figured they'd be here."

"Did you meet them, too, Alice?" Brigitte asked casually.

"I passed them on the stairs. They told me where to find Mom and Dad, but we didn't actually meet. Your son looks a lot like you, Robert."

"He's not my son. He's sort of a distant uncle or something."

"We thought he was your son, too. Very young for an uncle." Herb looked confused. "He introduced himself as Olivier de la Vallière."

Mooing came from the top of the curtains.

After a stunned silence, Romeo and Juliette charged into the room barking at the tops of their voices.

"Captain, desist this instant," demanded Brigitte. And the mooing stopped.

And so the tragic story of Mathilde, Olivier and Captain became general knowledge.

"Are we going to believe in ghosts now, Herby?" asked Gladys.

"I think we have to be open-minded about this, Glady."

Alice didn't want to be open-minded at all. She liked to stick with what she'd studied and felt sure there must be a perfectly rational explanation for all this, although for the moment she couldn't think of one.

"Yes, please," replied Andy to Robert's offer of yet another cognac.

"My ancestress, Louise de la Vallière, was a noted beauty of the 17th century and the first official mistress of Louis XIV. She bore four of his children but didn't care for court life and ultimately choose to spend the last years of her life in a convent."

Alice and her parents become more enchanted while Andy became more dismayed and helped himself to another cognac.

Guided by Brigitte, Herb had no difficulty driving them all back to Boulevard Beauséjour while Andy slept in the way back with his head on Alice's shoulder.

Pulling up in front of the apartment building, Herb said, "You all go on in. Andy and I'll go to La Rotonde and have a cup of coffee. We'll leave the car there."

A few minutes later, Andy was sitting opposite Herb with a large coffee before him and no way to escape. "It's time you and I had a little talk, son. You know, Scott Fitzgerald said, 'First you take a drink, then the drink takes a drink, and then the drink takes you.' I think that's where you are."

CHAPTER 15

Brigitte bolted the door of their apartment against the rest of the world, and Romeo dove onto the beige velvet sofa. He was allowed there on special occasions, and Brigitte and Romeo knew this was indeed one of those occasions. Brigitte turned on the fringed lamp and expectation sparkled through them before spreading around the little sitting room. Brigitte slid open the secret drawer, extracted the cards, sat down next to Romeo, stroked his head and unwound the red silk. Slowly she laid one card after another in a pattern on the table.

"Look at them! The star and the nine of Pentacles and the Wheel of Fortune. Oh, Romeo. Renewal, change and no more financial worries and the prospect of love!"

The sofa was not close enough to the cards for Romeo. He bounded onto the coffee table, belly flopped, slid spread-eagled across its highly polished surface, scattering cards in every direction before coming to an abrupt halt when Brigitte grabbed one of his back legs. He didn't care. Nor did she.

Again and again the cards said it. The Hermit had not made one appearance and the future was theirs. Brigitte stood and invited Romeo to join her. Hoisting him up and holding his left paw, they danced.

Five flights up, Gladys and Alice lay on the guest bed, going over the events of the day and deciding what furniture should go where in the Chateau. By the time Andy and Herb joined them, Andy had agreed to curtail his drinking and convinced Herb that his job prospects were excellent. In fact, he was expecting to receive a very interesting offer in the next few days, or so he told Herb.

"Just look at our two girls, Andy! Aren't we the luckiest ducks?"

"We certainly are, and you can start ticking off the days left at that school back home. Your future is here helping me run the chateau."

Andy sensed a mass hug-in about to happen and dashed to the kitchen and opened the fridge. "I'll 'curtail' starting tomorrow. I promise."

Alice joined him shortly afterwards. "Pour one for me, too, Andrew honey. Mom and Dad are off to bed."

Gladys lay awake dreaming of magical events unfurling at the chateau, while Herb descended into slumber. Sounds from the living room infiltrated her reveries, and although she was not deliberately listening, she could tell from the changing tones and clinking of glasses they were both drinking heavily. So much for Herb and Andy's little chat, she thought.

The following morning, Gladys's feigned busyness in the kitchen, intending to have a few words with Alice as they ate breakfast together. But that was not to be.

"Breakfast for me? Can't. I'm late. Love you, though. Have fun today." And she effortlessly slipped through Gladys's grasp. It wasn't intentional, or perhaps it was, a little. Gladys carried the coffee and toast intended for Alice to Herb. He was a tea man in the morning, but what the heck.

In was uncanny how often Henri happened to be crossing the Jardin du Ranelagh at the same time as Alice, even when, like today, she was later than late. Alice was walking and talking on her cell to Cynthia, telling her about Chateau de la Vallière, and was annoyed to see him making a beeline for her. "I'll call you later. My boss is bearing down on me."

"Bonjour. You're looking ravishing today. Paris must agree with you."

Alice smiled, "Bonjour, Henri." Others in the office greeted their colleagues with a kiss or handshake, but she was American and didn't.

"I've booked dinner in Berlin at a little place away from the conference venue where we can forget work."

"That sounds like fun. Lucky for me you'll be there to show me the town. Can't wait to see Berlin, and I'm looking forward to hearing you speak. What is the title of your paper?"

"'Fundamental Challenges and Post-Crisis Indications in an Asymmetric Environment'. More interesting for the economists than for the philosophers, perhaps, but extremely pertinent, nevertheless." On reaching the Phaye Institute entrance, Henri placed his palm against Alice's back to guide her through the door and up to the point where their office locations forced them apart.

Seeing Alice walk past her open office door, Yvette put down the press release she was editing on the Berlin conference, 'Imagining the Future Going Forward'. She decided she had to be more explicit with respect to Henri's reputation, fearing allusion and subtlety had not penetrated Alice.

At the same moment, Alice, convinced that Yvette and Henri required a little more of her matchmaking, took action.

Both women, bearing two coffees each, crossed in the corridor. They laughed at the coincidence and went to Alice's office, where Yvette put down her coffees on the desk and shut the door before taking a seat.

"I'm not one to gossip, Alice, but I think you ought to know that Henri can be a little difficult when on his own with women."

"I noticed. But you know, even the most confident man can be struck dumb in certain situations. Sometimes a little encouragement is required."

"I'm not sure encouragement is what he needs, Alice."

"Well, I think he does. He's at ease with me, so perhaps I can give him the courage he needs."

"You should think carefully before doing anything you might regret."

"Rest assured, Yvette, this isn't my first time. I've had a lot of success with romance. My favorite Rumi quote is: As you start to walk out on the way, the way appears. Leave everything to me."

Yvette left Alice's office puzzled. Who was this Alice? And what was she up to?

Pleased with her matchmaking, Alice sat at her desk and concentrated on visualizing Yvette and Henri's wedding taking place at La Vallière. "When love and skill work together, expect a masterpiece." Alice quoted John Ruskin aloud.

When Andy awoke he could tell his in-laws were still in the apartment and could hear enough of their conversation to know they weren't going to leave without an itinerary written by him. All he wanted was to pull the covers over his head for a couple of hours, but he gritted his teeth and threw on his terry cloth robe.

"Hi Andy, there's fresh coffee. Don't the French know how to start the day? These *'pains au chocolate aux amandes'* - did I say that correctly? - are yummy, yummy, yummy. And Herby gets on so well with Madame at the bakery."

Gladys beckoned Andy to his throne, and there he sat like an obedient schoolboy as Gladys bustled to and fro placing coffee, along with scrambled eggs, five or six varieties of leftover cheese, croissant, baguette, and orange juice on the ironing board, which she had lowered to a more convenient table height.

"Just think of it, Andy, we will be breakfasting together every day at the chateau. Birds singing, windows open and Edith Piaf on the radio. Herby has ideas about how to keep those wild pigs in check, too."

Andy knew Gladys and Herb were kind, thoughtful and well meaning, but no way could he endure the three days of Alice's business trip alone with them, much less have them be any part of a chateau venture. He had to wiggle out.

Grabbing a map of Paris, Andy circled the main attractions. "Is that the time? I'm already late. Sorry to eat and run, but I know you'll understand. Couldn't say 'no' to a meeting about a job, could I? Here, I've marked what you should see."

Andy showered and headed straight out for Patrick's, in need of grooming and advice. And like Alice, he'd slipped through their grasp.

"'Allo, Handy. What *can* I do?"

"I need the name of your tax accountant and your travel agent. And a shampoo and brushing."

"You're in luck." Patrick held his arm out to a dark-haired lady having the finishing touches put on her *coif* in the next chair over. "My travel agent is right here. Madame Ronze, may I present Handy 'Arreese, my American friend and client."

"Bonjour, Monsieur 'Arreese. How can I help?"

Andy explained he wanted two tickets for Berlin on Wednesday in the late afternoon, hotel reservations at the conference center and ground transportation in Berlin with English-speaking drivers. He took her card and said he would call her with the name of the hotel as soon as possible.

He then leaned back and put his aching head into Patrick's capable hands. "Patrick, listen. I don't want to buy a chateau. I really *can't* buy a chateau. But my wife and my in-laws and my landlady and her dog and the real estate agent and the owner of the chateau and his daughter and his cook and his butler and probably our best friends, the Lecerfs, all want me to buy a chateau. I need a tax accountant to say why it would be impossible for me to own a chateau even if I wanted to."

"Never worry. I know the right man for you. Nothing is *ever* possible according to Monsieur Framboise."

"I knew I could count on you. And something else calls for your genius. Alice's mother must have a total makeover on Wednesday. You know hair, make-up, clothes, the works. How long does it take for a complete job?"

"Most of the day."

"Good. I can get her here early, but she and her husband have to go to Berlin. Can you check with Madame Ronze what time we would have to leave for the airport? I'll be driving them and can come with the suitcases and pick her up here."

"Very good. It will be a pleasure."

Andy left Patrick's improved and relieved and went to La Rotonde for Wifi and coffee. After the man-to-man chat with Herb yesterday, Andy had vowed to himself he would indeed fill his days with worthwhile activities and job hunts, but today was out for Herb-approved activities. Tomorrow, Andy would pursue Herb's ideal of manly achievement, but today's most pressing tasks were to recoup his recent losses on Boulevard Jules Sandeau and get in touch with his new tax advisor.

While enjoying his cheeseburger and a half bottle of Bordeaux, Andy called Monsieur Framboise and fixed an appointment for Wednesday morning. He also called Yvette to ask the name of the convention hotel in Berlin.

"I have a surprise planned for Alice, so don't tell her I called. She leaves early Wednesday morning, right?"

"Yes. Her flight leaves Orly at six-fifty. Handy, I am so delighted you have a surprise planned for Alice in Berlin. She seems like the kind of person who loves surprises. And she deserves a big one."

"You've got her pegged already, Yvette. And this'll be a whopper."

Before the connection was cut, Andy could hear Yvette humming a little tune.

Next, Andy texted Christophe. 'Please arrange a tennis game for Herb Wednesday morning. Got to tire that guy out and send him to Berlin. '

Three hours later, Andy bounded back into La Rotonde. "A bottle of your favorite champagne for me, Didier. And pour a glass for yourself."

"Can't drink on the job, Monsieur 'Arreese, but I appreciate the offer. Madame Barbier and Romeo are on the terrace. Would you like me to serve the champagne there and bring two glasses?"

"Great idea."

Andy found Brigitte and Romeo and sat down, beaming. "I know you don't approve of poker, but I had a huge win today."

"I beg you, end on a high note and make this your last game. A big win is rare, as you know, so please don't push your luck."

"Let's just enjoy the champagne."

"Well, hello, you two." Gladys's smiling face appeared above the hedge. She was wearing the mother-of-pearl glasses. "May I come and join you?"

"Please do." Andy stood up and helped Gladys into her seat. "Where's Herb?"

"He went to see your friend Patrick to have a haircut. He's afraid of green streaks, but I told him not to be such a sissy."

Didier brought another glass and poured champagne for Gladys.

"Gladys, I've planned a little surprise for Alice. I've

got tickets and hotel reservations for you and Herb to go to Berlin, and I'm treating you to a makeover at Patrick's Wednesday morning in honor of your first trip to Germany."

"Oh, Andy! Did any woman *ever* have a better son-in-law? I definitely think *not*! I think I'll ask for blue streaks. What do you think, Brigitte? How would I look with blue streaks?"

"Isn't that an American expression? Talk a blue streak?"

"Oh, yeah, you're right. I'd better stick to green. Anyway, I love matching mother-daughter things, don't you? I really, really wish I could find another pair of these mother-of-pearl frames for Alice."

Brigitte and Andy looked at each other and nodded.

CHAPTER 16

Brigitte and Romeo were persuaded to come for cocktails *chez* Harris. Once Andy had made one of the boxes comfortable with a cushion and they were seated, Andy went around the room asking what each one of them had done during the day. He then expected someone to ask him the same, but the conversation moved on to the Chateau de la Vallière instead. No one bothered to ask Andy as everyone assumed he had done nothing more than go to La Rotonde.

He was not going to be denied his prepared speech. "As for me, this morning I prepared soup for the homeless at Notre Dame and taught English at a refugee center, and I took one of the kids to a museum."

Brigitte and Alice looked surprised but kept quiet. Gladys said, "Herby and I visited Notre Dame today, and we didn't see a soup kitchen, did we?"

"It's not at the Cathedral. It's in the deanery a few blocks away." Andy congratulated himself on his quick thinking as he took another drink, quite forgetting to offer to refill any other glass until prompted by Alice.

"What museum did you go to?" Herb asked. "I bet we were there, too. I think Glady and I went to every museum in Paris today."

Andy knew he should have thought of this. After all, he had circled the museums with a red marker.

"Palais de Tokyo," he said hoping it was one they'd missed.

"*What* did you *think* of that exhibition?" Gladys wanted to know.

Even though bullshitting about art had been his livelihood, at the moment he was taken aback by the question. He was expecting Herb's approval of a day well spent. He was unprepared and had no idea what was on at the Palais de Tokyo. He'd just have to fake it.

"I thought it was very interesting. The French are masters at the art of display, and only in Paris would the work be so sensitively presented and lit. Any artist is honored to be exhibited at the Palais de Tokyo. They have such avant-garde curators. Amazing, really." And he raised his glass to his lips.

"Just looked like a bunch of shoes to me." Herby said, looking at Andy askance.

"There are shoes, and there are shoes. The retrospective of Roger Vivier would be a drag to most kids. Only a French kid would like it. Good for you, Andy, for taking the chance to go there." Andy wanted to hug Gladys for trying to protect him.

"Let's go to La Gare for a change. Andrew, I have their card on my bedside box. Would you be an angel and give them a ring and see it they can give us a table for five in ten minutes?" Alice wanted to protect Andy, too.

"Make that a table for four. Romeo and I have a big day tomorrow and need our beauty sleep." Brigitte wanted no part of this. What had gotten into Handy to lie like this? It wasn't like him at all.

That Monday night at La Gare was slow. But Andy was on a high, and even before they were shown downstairs to their table in the garden, he ordered a magnum of Dom Perignon. When it was brought to the table, he said, "No, make that the Rosé 2003, if a place like this has such a fine wine."

Fortunately, the wine waiter did not understand the insult and came back with the Magnum. Looking very embarrassed, he said in a low voice that only Andy could hear, "Sorry, Monsieur, but I must tell you the price before I open the bottle to make sure you know how much it is. One thousand Euros."

Andy answered in a voice that carried well beyond their own table, "One thousand Euros is a bargain for this noble vintage."

Andy tasted the Champagne and nodded his approval. Gladys indicated that she only wanted a taste; Alice, the same. "Come on, Alice. I don't want to drink this whole thing by myself."

Herb said in a voice as loud as Andy's, "Noble vintage? Too grand for me. Pour that for the big-shot volunteer, and bring me a magnum of Coke, please." Alice had never heard her father be sarcastic before.

Andy and Herb got louder and louder as Alice and Gladys shrank smaller and smaller. Herb ended up telling Andy to stop showing off, and they walked home in silence, Andy needing Alice's steadying arm. He had finished the entire magnum alone.

Alice helped Andy to bed before she tapped on her parents' bedroom door. "Come on in, Sugarfoot."

"Mom and Dad, you know this isn't like Andrew. I think he's worried about the closing on our house tomorrow. He needs that money to buy the Chateau, and he's just nervous."

"Nervous, maybe, but with no job and all this drinking, I don't like it one bit. When you get back from Berlin, we'll have a family pow-wow. And while you're gone, don't worry about a thing. Your mother and I will keep an eye on him for you."

Alice kissed her parents goodnight, and once she was out of the room, Gladys told Herb about the surprise trip to Berlin.

"I think you should go, but I'm going to surprise Andy by coming back here. This boy needs supervision."

In the kitchen, Alice sat down and cried as she sipped her way through a bottle of Prosecco.

Tuesday was tense. They politely walked on eggshells and spoke in subdued voices avoiding each other as much as possible. Andy did tell Herb about the tennis and made sure Gladys knew her makeover at Patrick's began at eight-thirty, but there was little other communication.

Wednesday morning, Andy went down early to get a taxi and helped Alice with her suitcase. He hated to see Alice upset and he promised to apologize to her parents, but once her taxi was out of sight, he rushed back upstairs. He left a note for Gladys and Herb, saying to leave their suitcases out and he would met them both at Patrick's at the end of the day and drive them to the airport. Then he went straight to La Rotonde, believing he couldn't safely go back until after Herb and Gladys had left for their appointments. He would make it up to them somehow.

As the taxi drove away, Alice pulled a white handkerchief from her handbag and delicately placed it first to the corner of her right eye and then to her left, gathering tears before they ruined her mascara. Her eyes met those of the elderly driver in the rear view mirror. They both reddened at being discovered. The driver had carried many parting lovers on his early shifts, and he still felt sad when the women were about his own daughter's age. This was no time for vapid conversation. He turned on the radio.

Alice allowed her head to fall back against the leather headrest. Breathing deeply, she closed her eyes and tried to think back to when Andy started drinking heavily. Why had she not noticed before now? This question was easily answered: because she drank with him. Why he was drinking was not so easy to answer.

By the time the taxi drew up to the airport terminal, Alice had determined how to make everything and everyone better. The taxi driver handed over her small case, and there was Henri striding towards her.

She smiled at Henri.

"Good morning, Alice. You look splendid," and before she knew it, he had kissed both her checks.

"Ooh la, la" said the taxi driver to himself, "straight from one to the other."

Although the flight was delayed, making them late for the start of the conference, Henri insisted on detouring from the fastest route to Berlin's center. He was eager to show Alice particular places and buildings and provided a rapid historical run through. He was indeed knowledgeable, and Alice was grateful. Henri took pleasure in Alice's gratitude, and his expectations for the evening expanded.

They checked into the hotel and registered at the conference together. Before they went their separate ways for the day, Henri suggested they meet in the hotel bar before going off to the "special little place" he knew. Alice said that would be wonderful.

Back at La Rotonde, Andy was sitting at his table with his computer, feeling a little better. Manu brought his double

coffee and *tartine*, and Andy composed his daily email to
Billy. "Bro, wish you were here something terrible. Herb and
Gladys don't translate into French. And don't worry, I'm not
going to buy a chateau. Just trying to keep smiling today. Call
you later. A."

Andy left for Monsieur Framboise's office, Herb walked to
the TCP for his game, and Gladys arrived at Patrick's all at
about the same time as Alice's flight landed in Berlin.

Gladys's smile lit up Patrick's salon. Giselle and all the
beauticians were gathered to greet her, as well as a young man
who would bring in the latest fashions. She sat in Patrick's
chair surrounded by the experts who were frowning at her
mousy brown hair flecked with gray.

Patrick dissuaded Gladys from trying green streaks. He
pronounced that she should be a honey blonde with a few
paler highlights, dark brown eyebrows, false eyelashes and,
bien sur, no glasses. The personal shopper wanted to know
her shoe size, the facialist questioned her on allergies. The
masseuse asked if she liked Thai or Swedish. The waxer was
there as well as the manicurist, pedicurist, make-up artist
and colorist and, of course, Patrick himself had the final say
about everything.

Gladys was whisked off by the *masseuse* to begin her day
of extreme beauty. Patrick met with the personal shopper,
who soon went in search of the wardrobe. It would be
mostly Armani, with a dash of Nina Ricci. And Ellie Saab for
evening, garnished with Caron scarves and perfumes. Two
daytime ensembles and one evening, under and outerwear,

with accessories to match. Andy had told Patrick to leave nothing to chance.

By five p.m., Herb could be seen dragging himself up Avenue Mozart after playing singles with almost every man at the TCP. He had held his own set after set, with fresh players coming at the end of each. All the good players had wanted a turn with him.

He turned into the salon, waved to Patrick and flopped down on the sofa. Everyone was fussing around a movie star, even Lulu was yapping excitedly. Herb picked up a magazine and flipped through it while waiting for Gladys.

"Herby! Herby!" The shout came from the glamorous stranger who moved with all the grace of a trained ballet dancer.

Herb looked up. The voice was hers and the smile. But nothing else. This magnificent vision of Parisian chic standing tall on dangerous shoes was his Glady. The alluring aroma of expensive perfume floated four feet beyond her. Herb was speechless. Rushing forward to hug his wife, at the last second, Herb swerved, remembering how sweaty he was and hugged Patrick instead.

Moments later, Andy double-parked, came in and saw Gladys surrounded by Patrick's team. She wore a lilac Armani suit with touches of lace. The skirt was above her knees. He'd never realized that Alice got her beautiful legs from her mother. She had on pale gray high heels and carried matching gloves and a tri-colored Celine bag, lavender, pale gray and pewter. Her hair was blonde, cut to just under her ears, and blown straight. She looked like Alice, not like Gladys.

The personal shopper was explaining, "This suit takes you from an elegant luncheon through cocktails and dinner. Perfect for a day of restaurants and shopping in Paris or London or Berlin."

Andy felt he had gotten his money's worth. This was a makeover worthy of the name. He thanked Patrick and all the assistants and escorted Gladys and Herb into the waiting Hummer, carrying a suitcase containing the new clothes.

Herb had not packed a bag as he did not intend to go, but Andy planned otherwise. Earlier that afternoon Andy had thrown some clothes together for him and put his passport in the envelope with the flight information. On the drive to Orly, Gladys entertained them with details of her day, interspersed with many thanks to Andy. Herb had not recovered his voice and just stared at his wife in shock. As they pulled up to Lufthansa, Herb managed to say, "I'm sick not to be going with you, Glady-honey."

"Oh, but you are, Herb, old buddy. I have your suitcase in the back, and *voila,* your passport and tickets."

Herb's voice was thick with emotion. "That was real thoughtful of you, Andy, but I'm still in my tennis get-up."

"Come on. Let's go." Gladys gave Herb a little push.

"God bless you, son," Herb called out as he followed Gladys with the bags.

Andy breathed a sigh of relief as he watched them go into the terminal but stomped on the brakes just in time. Out of the corner of his eye, he noticed a crowd gathering around Gladys and went in to see if he could help. "It's Julia Roberts," someone said to him. "Get in line if you want an autograph." He saw that she'd managed to keep the mother-of-pearl glasses.

Andy disappeared before they saw him, got in the car and dialed Alice's cell. Getting no answer, he called Brigitte, who answered on the first ring.

"Brigitte, let me take you out to dinner."

"Oh, Handy, I'm not dressed for dinner."

"It's dinner with you or Boulevard Jules Sandeau for me tonight."

"I'll be ready in an hour. Is Romeo invited?"

"Of course."

Putting the Hummer in gear, Andy unclenched for the first time in days and drove northward though the darkness to Boulevard Beauséjour.

CHAPTER 17

Gladys had to wake Herb when they landed in Berlin. "You sure are pooped after all that tennis, Herby-pooh."

"And you sure look beautiful. I want to show you off to Alice before I hit the hay."

Gladys wasn't sure what the time was, but it seemed quite late by the time they arrived at the Hilton Hotel. She had to shake Herb awake again.

The receptionist phoned Alice's room, but there was no response. He suggested trying the hotel bar as some delegates from the conference were there. Gladys went to the bar while Herb attended to the bags and said he would see her in his dreams. "Way past my bedtime," he said as he followed the bellman to the elevator, his black and red sneakers squeaking on the marble floor.

As promised, Henri had taken Alice to a cozy little place away from the other delegates. Earlier in the day he couldn't help himself searching for her at coffee breaks between sessions that for him seemed interminably long. She was always surrounded by admirers, and he had to console himself with the thought of dinner.

The hotel bar where they'd met at eight was a sumptuous affair, providing round tables for groups and red leather high chairs at the extensive bar. Couples wanting privacy could choose one of the curved banquettes set into the alcoves lining two sides of the ornate room. It was to one of these banquettes that Henri and Alice returned after dinner to enjoy one last drink.

Henri was surprised at how much Alice drank during dinner but had been more than happy to continue refilling her glass while not always refilling his own. Their initial conversation had ranged wide and, for him, had contained too much talk about Yvette, but as the evening progressed, Alice became more and more animated and easy to please. No longer did she withdraw from his meaningful lingering looks deep into her eyes. Henri was content. Even his tired anecdotes elicited her laughter. Having secured the room next to Alice's, he was prepared to bide his time.

Now side-by-side on the banquette, he sat as close to her as possible, "I can't thank you enough for this evening."

"I enjoyed it, too. I've never had a boss take such an interest in my well-being."

"You're very important to me, and what else are friends for? Let's drink to friendship," and they raised their glasses yet again. This time as Alice lowered her glass, Henri ventured to put his arm around her shoulders. She did not object to his arm and turned to him, then raised her face. Just as their lips met, an acrobat landed right in front of their table.

Gladys had arrived in the almost empty bar and stood at the top of the two stairs leading to the sunken room and was surveying the scene, just as Henri made his move. Not hesitating for a instant, she slipped off her shoes, lifted her skirt and plunged into three *grands jetés,* down the stairs and across the room, landing and pirouetting as she removed her mother-of-pearl glasses and bowed, all the while clinging to her new Celine handbag. Of the few left in the bar, only the barman was not astounded. Henri's face twisted into an unattractive expression, and Alice jerked back before her astonishment turned to delight, followed by embarrassment.

"Henri, allow me to introduce my amazing mother, Gladys Blanes. Mom, this is Henri Frazier, my boss, who's been showing me the town."

Henri, being the sophisticated man he was, collected himself. "Mrs. Blanes, this is a great pleasure, though it's hard to believe you're Alice's mother. You look like sisters." He stood, held out his hand and made room for her to sit next to Alice. He reminded himself that he and Alice had adjoining rooms and charming her mother would only be to his advantage.

As Henri shook Gladys's limp hand, she felt grateful that Andy and Herb were not there. How lucky it was that she had flown through the air in the nick of time.

"Mom. I can't believe you're here, and I can't believe your *hair*. You must have spent all day *chez* Patrick."

"I did, Sugarfoot, and I'm a little tired. Daddy's upstairs and if your business has been concluded for the day, I think he would love to give you a kiss goodnight."

Henri didn't miss a beat. He stood again and said, "Go ahead, and I'll take care of the bill. I'm so glad to have met you, Mrs. Blanes. I'll see you in the morning, Alice. Goodnight, ladies."

Gladys bent down to pick up her shoes on the way to the lobby and whispered to Alice, "No one ever needs to know about this."

"Thank God you came when you did, Mom. I don't know what got into me."

"I think you and I will share a room, and Daddy will take yours."

Herb answered the door with half-closed eyes, dressed in the hotel bathrobe. "What do you think of your mother's makeover, Sugar-baby?"

"I think she just gets better and better. And you, too, Daddy." Alice gave her father a brief hug. The strong smell of alcohol was not lost on him.

"Herby, I want you to get dressed and go stay in Alice's room. I'm going to go with you and get her things to bring here. We girls need some private time together."

Herb was disappointed, but he knew this tone of voice. Objections would be useless. He did as he was told and was sleeping peacefully in Alice's room within fifteen minutes. He only vaguely heard the insistent knocking at the door. But the phone woke him up. "Hello. Hello?" No one was on the line. He hung up and drifted back to sleep, but five minutes later the phone rang again, and again there was no one on the line.

"Who is this American man in Alice's room? Has Andy come to Berlin, too?" Henri was full of frustration on the other side of the wall.

By the time Andy had dropped off the Hummer and was walking home, it was almost time to call for Brigitte. It was impossible not to notice the Harley with a sidecar parked right in front of the building, and he thought fondly of Billy who had the same model, but without a sidecar. Andy circled the bike pausing to grip the throttle handle and thought what an unusual sight it was in the sixteenth arrondissement of Paris.

Entering the lobby, he heard Romeo barking and decided to stop and warn Brigitte he would be picking her up in a few minutes. When she opened the door, Andy could see past her, and there, sitting on the beige velvet sofa, were Robert and Juliette.

Brigitte's cheeks were pink, and she smelled of Shalimar. Andy quickly kissed her and said, "Robert and Juliette, what a pleasant surprise to see you both in Paris."

Robert got up to shake his hand. "A spur of the moment trip. Juliette and I were out for a spin and thought since it's such lovely weather, we would come say hello to Brigitte and Romeo. I hope you won't mind if we join you for dinner."

Thinking on his feet, Andy said, "Your timing is perfect. I was coming to apologize to Brigitte as something has come up, and I can't make dinner. That's not your Harley out front, by any chance, is it, Robert?"

"Why, yes, it is."

"And the sidecar is for Juliette?"

"She loves it."

"I have to get a picture of this for my brother. Brigitte, will you be in the picture, too? And get Romeo in with Juliette. This'll be a classic."

Enthused by the idea, they all moved outside. Romeo couldn't wait to get in the sidecar with Juliette. With only a little encouragement, Brigitte sat astride behind Robert, donning the extra helmet and windbreaker he'd so thoughtfully brought.

"I bet Harley would pay a bundle for this photo," Andy commented.

"Since you aren't coming, and as we're all set, we'll just

say *à bientôt* and take off now." Robert revved the powerful engine and off they drove, hounds howling with happiness.

Andy watched them until they were no longer visible before getting out his phone. "Christo, Alice is in Berlin on business and Herb and Gladys are with her. I'm at a loose end. May I invite myself over?"

"Of course, *mon ami,* come right now. We're cooking up a storm. More than enough for all of us."

Andy ran up to the apartment, grabbed four bottles of Prosecco from the fridge and headed out for the Lecerfs on foot.

CHAPTER 18

Andy liked Cynthia. He liked her love of life, her empathy and her straight-talking, and that evening Cynthia had decided it was time for some straight-talking. Christophe would have preferred to discuss sports, but Cynthia wasn't having it.

Half way through dinner Cynthia asked, "How are you, Andy?"

"Fine, fine, fine."

"And Alice? How's Alice?"

"Fine as well. Just fine."

Cynthia looked at Andy. Always a little wary when he saw that look, Christophe went to the kitchen for something or other.

"I'll ask you again, Andy, because we both know, you're not fine. If you were, you wouldn't have drunk so much wine this evening. And we both know if Alice were here, she would have matched you glass for glass. "

"We don't drink that much. But you know, when in Rome...."

Cynthia waited.

"Okay. We're drinking more than we should."

Cynthia zeroed in, "I'm not sure you and Alice have come to terms with the miscarriages."

A knife twisted in Andy. "I do my best."

And rather than circle around the subject like he did with Alice, never daring to go closer for fear of hurting her, Andy allowed Cynthia to delve deeply. She was unafraid to make him confront the pain. "I think that you and Alice should see a grief counselor. Resorting to drink is not the answer. And you know it."

Cynthia's compassion as a friend and understanding as a professional was an overwhelming relief to Andy, and he spoke as he never had before. Cynthia didn't mention gambling and neither did he.

"You can come back now, Christophe," signaled the end of their conversation and the start of the serious question of how to beat Herb and Gladys at tennis.

Walking slowly back from the Lecerf's hours later, Andy didn't feel chastised at all. On the contrary, he felt hopeful for the first time in months. Cynthia made him see that he and Alice needed to talk to each other about their shared grief, comfort each other and make a plan for their future. He loved Alice, and whatever she wanted to do would be okay with him. Counselors or no counselors. There were options, after all.

Andy convinced himself that the drinking and gambling were related to the first miscarriage. This grief counseling will put a stop to all that, he thought. But it's really not that much of a problem. I'll cut back.

His phone pinged a message. It was from Sophie de la Vallière. She and Junior Viper had been in touch, and Junior wanted to meet up with Andy. He would be in Paris for ten more days.

"Well, how about that?" he chuckled to himself and then, "How about this?" as he saw the Harley and sidecar again parked outside his apartment building. Andy looked at his watch and whistled "La Vie en Rose" as he passed Brigitte's door.

Alice had passed a very troubled night in the king-size bed she'd shared with her mother. Gladys did not stir as Alice dragged herself from under the covers and dressed in the bathroom. She wrote a note and placed it on her cell phone next to the bed. They might need the phone, and she could manage without it for one day.

Her mother was right. Andy didn't need to know about her indiscretion, nor did her father, but she had to talk to Henri. And how could she face Yvette back in Paris? Alice skipped breakfast, for fear of running into Henri. She preferred to have the embarrassing conversation with him later at the conference.

Henri's presentation was to be the first of the morning. Due to falling back to sleep after his morning call, he, too, had decided to pass on breakfast. But they both needed coffee and came face-to-face much earlier than either would have wished. Alice immediately reddened to the blonde roots of her green-streaked hair. Henri, experienced in such situations, immediately broke into a smile.

"Good morning. Are your parents well this morning? Has Andy surprised you by coming, too? When you don't work, it's so easy to arrange such things."

Alice could feel the back of her neck becoming damp. "No. Andy's not here. And my parents are very well, thanks."

Henri wanted to ask about the man in her room last night, but even he could not find the right words before Alice launched into her rehearsed apology. Touching her arm, Henri interrupted her right away.

"No need to apologize. We had a good evening together. We should do it again very soon." Henri, in turn, was cut short by being told it was time for his speech, and Alice was relieved to see his back.

Alice didn't hear a word Henri said, even though she was seated in the fourth row and felt his eyes coming to rest on her more than once. Instead, it was her mother's words that circled in her mind. "No one's perfect, Sugarfoot. You're allowed to make mistakes. Nothing happened, so why upset Andy? Forget about it." But she couldn't forget it. She had let Andy down, yet again. Her perceived failings flooded her reason. Okay, not being able to have children was not her fault, but last night was.

Gladys didn't realize Alice was gone until she was woken by Herb's knocking on the door. "Come on, Glady, get dressed. Berlin's waiting for you."

"I'm ready for Berlin, but what to wear?" Gladys wiggled her multi-colored toes at Herb. They were painted all the joyous colors of M and M candies.

Before Herb had a chance to comment, Alice's cell started to ring. "She's forgotten her phone," said Gladys.

Herb saw the note, "She's left it for us, and it's Andy calling. Andy! Great to be here."

Andy was surprised, "Where's Alice?"

"She didn't trust us alone in Berlin without a phone. And thanks for getting me here. I've organized a grand tour of Berlin for us, but Glady can't decide what to wear. She has two more minutes before I drag her downstairs in her sexy undies and confetti toes." As an afterthought he added, "this is Alice's phone, - well you know that, don't you?"

Then Gladys took the phone. "Andy, how can I ever thank you? And how can I choose from so many wonderful things to wear? I can't wait to wear the evening dress. It's perfect for entertaining at the chateau!"

Andy couldn't think of a suitable response. Hearing Herb in the background grumbling about wanting his breakfast saved him.

"I think you'd better get your man fed, Gladys. Have a great day."

Andy was hungry, too, but chose La Rotonde over the many possibilities that now filled the kitchen cupboards to overflowing, thanks to Herb. Besides, he wanted to check on that Harley downstairs.

It wasn't parked outside the building, but he could hear it. He was just in time to see Robert, with Juliette at his side, pealing off Boulevard Beauséjour. And wasn't that Brigitte and Romeo walking quickly away from him across the park? Andy sensed an ideal opportunity to tease Brigitte and marched briskly across the road into the park, cutting down the distance between him and his prey with every stride.

"*Bonjour*, Brigitte, what a delightful morning for a walk. It's interesting what one sees at this time of day."

Brigitte knew he had seen Robert. "*Bonjour*. Handy. Isn't this rather early for you?"

"I do believe you are blushing, and what's this? Romeo blushing, too?"

"Monsieur 'Arreese, don't you have somewhere to go?"

They both laughed. He touched her arm, raised his eyebrow and invited her for a coffee after her walk and went on his way.

Andy's infectious smile spread among the staff in La Rotonde where breakfast and computer were delivered to his table along with a small vase of yellow tulips. Manu offered to connect the transformer.

"Thanks, Manu, but I think I almost have the hang of this – I'm a quick learner."

He scrolled down the unopened emails checking to see if there was anything interesting. He then hesitated between an email from Billy and one from his New York attorney, certainly about the sale of the brownstone.

"Come on, baby, don't let me down." He clicked on the latter. Unable to confront the words face on, he turned sideways, feigning interest in the stream of workers rushing to their offices. He skimmed the message from the corner of his eye, ready to look away if the words were disappointing. The words "transaction completed" and "money transferred" jumped out big and bold. "Bingo! Waahoo, Manu. A large Irish coffee, please."

"Shall I bring another *tartine* as well?" asked Manu. It was awfully early for Irish coffee in his opinion. Andy nodded and re-read the message slowly to make sure he'd got it right.

His next reaction was to pull out his phone to share this good news with Alice, but Herb had her phone, so that was out. He was still brimming with "transaction completed" euphoria when Brigitte arrived.

Andy picked her up and kissed her twice on each cheek. He would have kissed Romeo, too, if Romeo's legs had been longer.

"I can pay off all my debts! You can't imagine how good that feels."

"C'*est merveilleux*! I'm delighted for you. Good news comes in bundles, you know, and you'll have more soon, I predict."

"And what about you? I see there is no wedding band on your left hand this morning. I would like a complete explanation for that, if you please."

"Just order the coffee, Handy."

Back at the Hilton Hotel, Herb and Gladys caught up on the international news and tucked into their breakfast, returning to the buffet time after time.

"Hope I'm back with you tonight, Glady. Too much action in Alice's room. The phone kept ringing, and there was even some banging on the door."

Of course, Gladys knew exactly who would have woken Herb, but she was not about to say. "Maybe your neighbors were trying to shut up your snoring. Did you ever think of that?"

"How can I snore if they don't let me sleep?" whined Herb. Then in a more serious tone, he said, "We've got to talk to

Alice about her drinking. Even half-asleep, I could tell she was pretty far gone last night."

"You're right about that. And I think you should stay where you are for tonight and let me handle this."

Touring Berlin, Gladys tried hard to concentrate on the guide explaining the rich culture and history of the city but, like her daughter, the words were repeatedly drowned out by her own thoughts. What would she say to Alice? Everything she came up with sounded wrong. Too shrinky, or not shrinky enough. Too p.c. to make any sense, or not p.c. enough. In the end when they were finally alone in the room, she sat on the edge of the bed and dove right in.

"I thought you were happily married, Sugarfoot."

"I am, Mom." Clearly upset, Alice cast her eyes downwards as she sat in a chair near the window. "I had too much to drink last night. I told you, I don't know what got into me."

"I was vacuuming the other day and ran into ten wine bottles under your bed. There's been a lot of drinking going on since we arrived, and your fridge looks like an alcoholic dream."

"I know. I'm working long hours and just haven't gotten around to going to the supermarket yet."

"You've been here nearly four months, and Andy doesn't work. Can't he go?"

"I know. I know, Mom."

"I don't like to be a nag, but if you want to get pregnant, I think you should start looking at your nutrition. And cut back on your drinking."

Alice felt the sting. She stood up and stepped over to the window, turning her back on her mother. "I hate to tell you this, Mom, but there aren't going to be any children. At least not in the usual way. I've been seeing a fertility specialist. Three miscarriages in four years, and nothing at all in the last two. So you see, it doesn't matter about my nutrition."

"Oh, Sugarfoot, come here," was all Gladys could manage. Like the little girl she was Alice sank into her mother's arms and let herself be rocked gently back and forth. "I know how it hurts. Why do you think you're an only child? And so treasured after we waited so long."

CHAPTER 19

With the weight of his debts off his shoulders and buoyed by the Irish coffee, Andy bounded along the streets. He was meeting Sophie outside the Franklin D. Roosevelt metro station before going to see Junior Viper. To be sure the thought of meeting Junior again after such a long time made him a little nervous, but he was determined that it wouldn't ruin his day.

He didn't recognize the strictly dressed woman with her hair tied back waving to him outside the station. But his natural Texan friendliness had him grinning and waving enthusiastically in her direction.

"Thanks for coming early. I want to ask you something before we see Junior. It's a bit difficult, as you will see."

As long as it wasn't anything about Congressman Viper or *Cool,* Andy was happy to oblige. He was relieved when Sophie asked how much Andy thought she could get for her Viper paintings. She and her brother were sad that their father was selling La Vallière, and although he had never said anything, she thought it might be a financial decision.

"It costs a bomb to run La Vallière, and if selling the paintings means Papa can keep it, then I would like to sell them."

The words "costs a bomb" rang alarm bells in Andy's head, and he almost missed what Sophie said next.

"Of course it's impertinent to ask you such a question as you are the very person planning to buy La Vallière, but you are the 'Viper expert', and these are paintings that have never been exhibited before."

"I don't think you're impertinent at all, Sophie. I'd say the paintings are worth about $200,000, each. That's just a guess, and on the high side, but I've never seen better Vipers. They'll always fetch the high end of what his paintings go for, and if the bottom doesn't fall out of the Contemporary market, they could be worth a lot more in a few years' time."

"That could make a big difference to the family finances and save the chateau for a while at least. I hope you won't be too disappointed, given all your plans. But you know France is overflowing with chateaux for sale at the moment, and you'll easily find another one."

"I'm not so sure I'm suited to chateau life. Your family keeping La Vallière could get me out of a lot of trouble. But please forget I said that."

They arrived outside Le Matignon, and Andy pushed open the door. They chose a table near the door, and Junior bustled in a few minutes later.

"Andy, my man! Good to see you." He shook Andy's hand and bent down to kiss Sophie on the top of her head. "Hope I didn't keep you guys waiting." Sitting down between them, he opened a worn leather document case.

"Sophie already knows what I'm going to say, so let me cut to the chase. I bought *Cool* a few months ago. I want you to be part of starting *EuroCool* with Sophie here as house counsel and Chapieski as Editor. I haven't talked to Chapieski yet, but I know he isn't happy at the paper, and I think it's time he got into admin. I want you to be our critic in Europe and come to New York for the big shows. You're the best there is, and I can offer a twenty percent increase on what you made at *Cool,* plus an expanded expense account."

Junior set out his plans, and Andy could feel his adrenalin begin to pump. He could see a big change in Junior and wondered what had happened. "Junior, this is big news. I had no idea. I saw Stan recently, and he didn't say anything about your buying *Cool.*"

"That's because he doesn't know yet. It'll be official next week. I had my reasons for not letting it leak. Now tell me, are you in? But you're going to have to promise me not to write any reviews of shows you haven't viewed!"

"I guess that cat's out of the bag," Andy said. From Sophie's face it was clear she knew the whole backstory, which was a huge relief to Andy.

"I own *Cool* now, so I've seen all the records. But you're still the guy with the best instinct for Contemporary. I want you for *EuroCool*, and if you want to move back to New York, I want you at *Cool*. Nobody touches you, Andy, but you have to pay attention. No more screw-ups. What's your answer?"

"You've made me an offer I can't refuse. But what's going on with you, Junior? Besides the magazine?"

"About a year ago my old man married a thirty-one-year-old Russian beauty, and his life is a living hell. So now he has no time to get on my case. Funny, I never realized how bad it was. I mean, I knew, but not the extent. I'm finally a free man."

Andy nodded. "Awesome." At the same time a mist descended on Andy's clear conscience. Did Junior know about the pact between him and the Congressman?

Andy phoned Alice from the back of the taxi taking him home. There was so much to tell her and all good, but Herb's tired voice answered. "I'm still in charge of the phone, Andy. Not in charge of my feet, unlike Glady of course, who's still lively as a Mexican jumping bean and googling restaurants for tonight. Hey, do you think we should invite Alice's boss to join us? He took Alice out last night. I'll find out his room number and call him." Gladys said something in the background, but Andy couldn't make out what.

Andy left a message for his twin. "Got great news for you, Billy-Bob. Find out why."

Andy was buzzing. He was not just on his way back up, he was there and ready to roll. Back at *Cool,* and the Congressman experiencing serious karma kickback. *Rock on.*

Tomorrow, he determined, he would re-enter the art world with a bang. The prospect sent shivers up his spine.

As the taxi passed La Rotonde, Andy leaned forward placing his hand on the back of the passenger seat. "Not Boulevard Beauséjour, Monsieur. Boulevard Jules Sandeau instead, *s'il vous plait.*" He did feel a little guilty breaking his promise to himself and Brigitte but, hey.

Much poorer, much later and after numerous drinks, it took Andy five attempts to tap out the code before the front door gave way. He lurched into the lobby and stumbled noisily past Brigitte's door, telling himself over and over to be quiet. Once safely inside his apartment, he mumbled something about wanting to tell Alice, fell onto his bed and passed out in his clothes. He never heard the phone ringing.

A few hours later, as the sun rose, he heard it, and it was Alice. Lying horizontally across the bed with a sock covering his eyes, he listed the gains without mentioning the losses of the previous day. Alice was ecstatic about *EuroCool,* but insisted they should still take on the chateau, as she thought Andy and her parents loved the idea.

"Got to go, Andrew-honey. I'm on in a few." Her presence receded too quickly back to Berlin.

"Oh, God, the chateau," thought Andy.

The phone rang again almost immediately, and he arranged to meet Sophie at La Rotonde to draw up his contract.

He then threw off his clothes and snuggled back under the covers, only to be woken two hours later by another bell.

"What the hell's going on today?"

Grabbing his robe off the doorknob, he opened the door to Brigitte and Romeo. They had given up waiting downstairs to catch him on his way out.

"Handy, you know we must talk. We saw you on Boulevard Jules Sandeau yesterday."

"What time is it? I have a meeting at eleven."

She showed him her watch. It read ten forty-five. "You're going to miss it."

"I can't." He left them at the open door and ran back into the bathroom.

Brigitte and Romeo invited themselves inside but stood in the hall between the bathroom and Andy's bedroom as he ran back and forth.

"How could you, Handy? How could you?" Brigitte chided Andy but he offered no defense until fully dressed and ready to leave.

He stopped, gave her a big kiss and said, "My future's going to be fine. I've been offered a great job, and I won't want to gamble anymore. You'll see it in the cards. Have a look and I'll come by this afternoon." And he left her standing in his apartment.

He was late entering La Rotonde, but not as late as Sophie, and was able to politely wave aside her apologies. Their *EuroCool* business was easy to conclude, which was a good thing as Sophie, although professional, was clearly distracted.

She put the papers back in her soft leather briefcase. "I saw Papa in the distance on my way here. I recognized the Harley and Juliette in the sidecar. Do you think he came to see Brigitte?"

Oops, thought Andy. Trying not to let the cat out of the bag, he said, "You'll have to talk to your father about that."

"I thought so."

There followed a flurry of comments on the virtues of both Robert and Brigitte as though Andy and Sophie were brokering a suitable marriage. The addition of Romeo and Juliette's merits completed the perfect merger.

That settled, Sophie joined Andy in ordering a cheeseburger, and they toasted the future with sparkling water. Andy asked for the Hummer to be brought as he was off to the airport to meet the Lufthansa flight, and Sophie left for her appointment with Junior and Stan. There was just enough time for Andy to down a small cognac before jumping into the driver's seat.

CHAPTER 20

Having learned how to squeeze the Hummer into tight spaces, parking at the airport was child's play. Andy was going to be sad to give up the rental in a few days' time, but a car really wasn't necessary in Paris, and he thought he might try a hybrid the next time they needed one.

Gladys and Herb arrived with a flourish and presented Andy with a 3D puzzle of the Brandenburg Gate. Alice made a funny face mirroring Andy's before giving him a kiss, and Henri held out his hand.

It would have seemed churlish if Henri had refused a lift in the Hummer, but he made sure he sat as far back as possible to distance himself from Gladys. Having sat next to her on the flight from Berlin was more than enough for him. The prospect of spending more time with Gladys was substantially reducing his infatuation with Alice. Gladys knew what she was doing.

Henri and Alice climbed down from the Hummer outside the Phaye Institute as they had work to do, and Henri followed Alice into the building. "Nice man. Doesn't say much," commented Herb as they pulled away.

The Harley was back outside the apartment building. When told it belonged to Robert de la Vallière, Herb asked, "Do you think he'd take Glady and me for a spin round gay Paree?"

Gladys smiled weakly in agreement. Once in the lobby she said, "I'm parched after all that talking. I need some water." They rose to the fifth floor in silence.

"Are you sick or something?" asked Herb as he followed her into the kitchen.

That afternoon, Romeo and Juliette were stationed near the slightly open door of Brigitte's apartment. Both woofed as Andy raced downstairs into the lobby. Brigitte was able to stop him on his way out to do battle with the Internet provider.

She leaned close and whispered, "Don't mention the cards, Handy," then, in a louder voice, invited him in for tea. Andy could spare a few minutes.

He had often thought Brigitte's salon dark but that day it oozed light and happiness and next to the teacups was a plate of miniature chocolate eclairs.

Robert stood and greeted him with a warm handshake.

"I'm getting used to seeing your Harley outside," Andy said and then wished he hadn't because it sounded suggestive.

"To be honest, I expect you'll be seeing it outside quite a bit, for a short time anyway." Robert said and cleared his throat.

"I'm afraid I'm going to have to disappoint you about the chateau, Andy. I was selling it because I was lonely, and, well, I don't think I'm going to be lonely anymore." He moved closer to Brigitte and took her hand in his. "Brigitte has just agreed to become my wife." Before Andy had time to say anything, Robert continued. "I know what you're thinking - it's all very quick, too quick. But we both know it's right for us, don't we Brigitte."

Brigitte's sparkle spoke for her.

Andy wasn't a hugging kind of person, but he couldn't help himself.

Robert produced the champagne he had brought "just in case", and Brigitte replaced the teacups with flutes. Andy turned down Robert's kind offer to help him find another suitable chateau but said he'd be interested in the gatehouse if Robert would consider renting it.

Brigitte looked at Robert, although her words were meant for Andy, "You never know because we do plan to open the chateau for weddings and other joyous events. There's that beautiful 19th century chapel, after all."

As he was about to leave, Andy remembered Herb's request. Robert laughed and agreed to give Gladys and Herb a spin in the Harley. "Only if one of them is prepared to wear Juliette's helmet. I'm on my way to see Sophie and tell her our happy news." He looked at his watch. "I can pick them up about six-thirty. Warn Gladys to wear something warm. It gets quite chilly when the sun goes down."

Andy lagged behind, hoping to get a look at the cards once Robert had left, but Brigitte shooed him out saying she was much too busy now, but maybe tomorrow.

The Internet would have to wait. Andy bounded back up the stairs to the fifth floor and hunted everywhere he thought Alice might have put the receipt for the chairs, but to no avail. He even looked under the bed, where he came face to face with the bag of empty bottles.

Wondering what all the fuss was about, Gladys stopped unpacking, "What's up?"

"Looking for the receipt for the chairs."

"I put all the papers I found when vacuuming in a kitchen drawer."

"I'm in luck," he said reading the address on the invoice. "The shop is just around the corner. We have a lot to celebrate, Glady, and we don't have enough chairs," and he was off out of the door with the bag of empty bottles. Andy hesitated a second at the top of the stairs. "Did I just say 'Glady'?"

Back in the kitchen, Herb looked at Gladys. "Here we go celebrating again."

It was too late for Andy to go to Boulevard Jules Sandeau and still be back when Alice got home, although he was itching to go and feeling guilty about the itching. He looked at his watch after pushing the last bottle into the bottle bank, "It's such a good day. I would surely win," he said to the empty plastic bag as he dumped it into a nearby bin.

It took an enormous amount of will power to direct himself along the sidewalk and into the furniture shop where he ordered two more chairs, a sofa and a table to replace the ironing board. He then congratulated himself by popping into La Rotonde for one, that turned into three, cocktails on the way home.

Although it had been a good day, Andy knew there was a vast black cloud overhead ready to burst. Okay, he didn't need money for La Vallière, Robert and Brigitte had solved that problem, but how was he to explain there was almost no money from the sale of the brownstone? Alice had loved the chateau and was probably ready to love another one. And there were no Vipers.

Of course, he wouldn't tell Alice until her parents had gone back to Des Moines. One rebuke from Herb was sufficient for this visit. He chuckled when he remembered claiming he was expecting a good job offer, and then a few days later he actually had an excellent one. "I don't need tarot cards to predict *my* future," he muttered.

"What's that you said about the future?" It was Christophe. "They'll put a plaque on this table with your name on it soon."

"Christo! Thanks for tiring out Herb for me the other day."

Christophe listened to Andy's news before he commented, "But we both know there's still a large financial discrepancy. You're not gambling in Paris, are you?"

Andy was quick in replying, "Not like in New York." Christophe was a good friend, but Andy wasn't about to tell him about the trips to Boulevard Jules Sandeau.

Christophe wasn't hoodwinked. "So you're not only drinking like a fish, but gambling, too?" At times like these Andy preferred Cynthia. "I'll take your silence as a 'yes'."

"I don't drink that much, and anyway I could stop if I wanted to. And I don't gamble like I did in New York. Everything's under control. And for your information, I do come out on top quite often. I really don't need you on my back. It's bad enough having to listen to Brigitte."

"And how many times don't you come out on top? Often enough to have nothing to show after selling the brownstone?"

Andy remained defiantly silent.

"I should never have agreed to keep quiet about this. I was stupid to believe all your promises about France being a new start. *Merde,* Andy, I can live with Alice being angry when she finds out I knew all along but worse is the fact that Cynthia will never trust me again. I was crazy to sign as your guarantor on that bank loan here."

"You can't tell Cynthia."

"Give me one good reason why not."

An unpleasant conversation ensued between the two friends in which Andy managed to obtain a stay of execution regarding Cynthia until Alice's parents left for Des Moines in a few days' time. But true to the loyalty Christophe retained for Andy, he insisted they leave La Rotonde together, and he walked Andy back to his building, where he stayed outside until he was sure Andy had actually gone home.

CHAPTER 21

One of the two chairs and the coffee table, which Andy had ordered, arrived minutes before Brigitte and Robert. The sofa and second chair would take a few more days. It wasn't a problem. Andy was more than happy to sit on a box of books when he wasn't opening bottles, filling glasses and proposing toasts to the newly engaged.

"I'm sure Mademoiselle Dumont can find us another chateau nearby. Not as perfect as La Vallière, of course," Alice said.

"Then we'll all be neighbors," Gladys chimed.

"I hate to end this party, but I promised to take my bride-to-be to meet some of my cousins for dinner." Robert held his arm out to Brigitte.

The door clicked closed, and the party continued without them.

Out of consideration for Alice and Andy, Gladys and Herb told each other to keep quiet as they crept around the apartment early the following morning. But in truth both wanted Alice to get up. It was their last day in Paris, and their whispers became louder and louder until she emerged.

"There're still so many places to see, Sugarfoot. We've made a list and need to get going since we're playing tennis this afternoon."

"Christophe and Andy said they'd meet us at the tennis club." Herb interjected.

Andy appeared wrapped in his robe in time to hear this. There was no way he was going to the tennis club. He said he would meet them there just to please them, but he would make sure it became impossible for him to go. Once Herb and Gladys in their matching sneakers had set off with Alice, Andy went back to bed until hunger made him rise and dress. Bypassing all the food in the kitchen, yet again, he headed for La Rotonde.

The Harley was not outside the building. He checked up and down the street to see if it were nearby and spotted Brigitte returning from the park with Romeo.

"Just you and Romeo today?" Andy asked. They went back into her apartment, where Brigitte made coffee and chatted about the refurbishment of the chapel for the wedding.

Flowers, courtesy of Robert, graced every available surface in the room, and a thornless red rose was entwined in Romeo's collar.

"This is impressive," Andy said, looking around. "Good thing you've got so many vases."

"You'd be amazed at what I have tucked away."

Brigitte opened the hidden panel in the desk and brought out the tarot cards wrapped in their red silk scarf. She sat next to Andy on the sofa.

"I'm going to give you these cards, Handy. I know all I need to about my future, and if there's something horrible waiting for me, I don't want to know about it." Brigitte handed Andy a cup of coffee.

"Sophie called before Robert came back last night, welcoming me into their family. She said her brother Jacques had been worrying about Robert being isolated at the chateau and that he'll be delighted about our marriage. What more could I ask?"

Perhaps the fact that Brigitte had no children made family acceptance easy flashed through Andy's mind before he pushed it away. He mentioned that he and Sophie would be working together very soon launching *EuroCool.*

Picking up the tarot cards, Andy said, "I think you're trying to get rid of the cards, Brigitte. Don't want Robert knowing? Well, guess what. I don't want Alice knowing, either."

"Okay. Shuffle and cut into three." On seeing the cards laid out, Brigitte sat up and pursed her lips. "Do you expect me to repeat what these cards say?" she asked passing her palm over two of them. "Well, I refuse to, just like you refuse to stop gambling. It's your choice to continue, and it's my choice to quit worrying about you." She was clearly annoyed but pointed out that the health issue would soon be resolved and everything related to work was positive.

With the cards wrapped back in the red silk and put away, Brigitte's disappointment in Andy made light-hearted chat between them difficult. After a few minutes of unsuccessful conversation, Andy checked his watch.

"I've got to go. The rest of the furniture will be here any minute."

At the Tennis Club, Alice's phone pinged. "I'm afraid Andy won't be coming," she said after reading the text. "The *EuroCool* meeting is taking much longer than he thought it would."

Christophe had not expected Andy to join them at the Tennis Club, nor had he expected Alice to invite them back to the apartment for drinks. He felt compelled to ask whether Andy would be okay with that after having to spend most of the day in a meeting. Alice could think of no reason why he wouldn't be very pleased, and anyway Gladys wanted to show Cynthia all her new clothes. Andy's extravagance and irresponsibility about money, made obvious by this "make-over" angered Christophe.

"I hope you don't mind, Alice and Gladys, but I have less interest in fashion than Andy, and I have a family to support. So I'm going back to work." His tone was sharp. Cynthia looked up, concerned for Christophe, but taken aback by his insensitive choice of words. Christophe continued, "You go ahead, *ma chérie*, I'll see you at home."

Andy walked away from Boulevard Jules Sandeau neither up nor down financially. He knew he should feel guilty but he didn't and was elated to see Cynthia admiring Gladys's new wardrobe. The chatter of the three women about fashion and beauty was just what he wanted to hear. He felt like a hero for having provided their subject matter. They exclaimed over how beautiful Gladys looked and over what a thoughtful, generous and imaginative guy he was. If he had been a cat, he would have been purring.

"Here you are, Herb," said Andy handing him a glass of champagne, "Let's take the thrones and survey our beautiful women. Good job some of the boxes and the ironing board are gone. Would've spoiled our view."

Everyone raised their glasses to Gladys, who bowed graciously. Andy looked across at Alice and thought he noticed that she raised the glass to her lips but didn't drink.

"Have to find somewhere back home for you to show off those clothes, Glady-girl."

"Herby, I've decided I'm going to leave the lavender suit and the evening dress here so Alice can borrow them, and I can always wear them when we come back this summer. I'm taking that navy Armani pants suit, though. And you'd better take me someplace to wear it."

Soon the conversation turned to the Blanes' departure on the noon flight the following day. Cynthia would come over at eight in the morning with fresh croissants, and then Andy and Alice would drive them to the airport. Herb protested that Madame at the bakery would be denied a last meaningful conversation with him, but Gladys said the rest of the people standing in line while he had his French lesson would be pleased. Andy knew Christophe wouldn't be coming with the croissants.

Alice was sad to see her parents go through the barrier at the airport but once back in the car her mind turned to chateau hunting. It was no good. Andy couldn't let Alice go on making suggestions about what to do with the proceeds of the brownstone sale. He pulled off the main road and stopped the Hummer.

"Alice, there's something I have to tell you." Andy did not tell the whole truth, and he implied that his consideration for her was the reason for his previous silence. "I made some stupid investments, and they failed. I'm sorting it out, and when proceeds from the fracking come through, we'll be able to do whatever you want." Andy gave her a quick kiss and re-started the engine. "And I have to tell you, I never owned those Vipers. I should have made that clear. I'm sorry. They were on loan. But with all our oil money you'll be able to have as many Vipers as you want."

Alice was quiet for a short time and then reached out and placed her hand on Andy's thigh. The financial pressure explains his drinking, she told herself. Her exclusion, however, from his troubles had planted a kernel of doubt deep within her. What else had he been keeping from her?

CHAPTER 22

For the next few months, as spring turned to summer, life on Boulevard Beauséjour took on the rhythm of routine. Andy still had breakfast at La Rotonde, but with the WiFi connection up and running in the apartment, his computer arrived with him and stayed in the bag at his feet while he read the newspaper. He never stayed long before heading for his office in the Marais. *EuroCool* would hit the art world with a big splash in January, and Junior was impressed with the pace of their progress.

Alice never noticed Henri's absence as she crossed the park in the mornings, nor did she miss his visits to her office. Her reason for suddenly disliking alcohol, however, did become apparent. She was of two minds about whether to tell Andy she was pregnant again, as he would surely worry. She decided to wait and talk to Cynthia about this and her other concern. Meanwhile, she would concentrate on getting Yvette and Henri together.

Pursuing her mission, Alice sought out Yvette, and they left for lunch. As they were waiting at the light to cross

La Muette, Yvette nudged Alice, "Look, over there." She indicated a table on the terrace of La Rotonde. "It's Henri with the new intern. Alice, you're safe. He's moved on."

"What are you talking about?"

"Surely you must have realized what was going on."

"Between you and him?"

Yvette started laughing. "Heavens, no. What little there was between us was over years ago. Now I spend my time telling him to grow up."

Alice didn't quite believe this. "Then, why does he keep coming to see you? You're always talking with him in the hall."

"Not any more. And it wasn't me. It was you he wanted to see. I was forever jumping out of my office and telling him to go away. Look at him. He's such a smooth operator."

"But what about that time I saw you together in the park and the evening at my apartment? And the time the chairs were delivered?"

"We were arguing about you in the *Jardin,* and I refused to let him be in your apartment alone with you. He was very cross."

Alice was silent for a moment before she slipped her arm through Yvette's. "I almost made a complete fool of myself in Berlin, but my mother saved me." When the light changed, they crossed. As they passed Henri's table, they waved. Henri grinned and waved back.

Later that same day Alice arranged to meet Cynthia in the Jardin du Ranelagh after work. She could confide in Cynthia, and at six p.m. it was a lovely day and the light was still strong."

Cynthia had been to Patrick's where she'd had another pink streak added to her hair. She was surprised to see Alice with shorter hair.

"What's happened? I go pinker, and Patrick gives you a cut that makes you look more beautiful than ever plus all the green streaks are gone."

Alice couldn't help smoothing her hair and took a sip from her water bottle before telling Cynthia her good news. "I just don't know whether to tell Andrew yet. He needs to focus all his energy on *EuroCool* and not have to worry about me. And he will worry."

"You should tell him. Of course, he'll be over-protective and worried, but given your history, you need to be extra careful. Andy will make sure you take it easy."

"It's amazing that this happened now. I gave up all hope when we left New York, and here we are only six months later."

"I'm so happy for you. Everything will be fine. Doctor Lalanne is the best, and he'll take perfect care of you."

Alice's expression became serious. "I do have another concern. Mom pointed out to me how much Andy and I drink, and for the past two months, I haven't had a drop of alcohol. But I have noticed how often Andy is under the influence. What do you think? I mean, as a friend and as a professional?"

Cynthia did not hold back. "To tell you the truth, Christophe and I have been worried about both of you ever since you arrived in Paris. We all drank in New York, but nothing like what you guys are drinking here. I'm glad you've had the sense to stop."

"Why didn't you say something?" Alice asked.

Cynthia agreed that she or Christophe should have said something, but, "It's not an easy subject, and I did bring it up with Andy while you were in Berlin."

"What did he say?"

"He didn't want to discuss the drinking. I suggested you consider grief counseling for the miscarriages."

"He never mentioned that to me."

"It's no longer relevant and my guess is that he'll cut back on his drinking during your pregnancy. There are places where he can get help if the problem continues. Do you know Andy and Christophe are having a little tiff right now? I'm pretty sure it has to do with Andy's drinking."

Alice was aware that they hadn't been meeting at the Tennis Club since her parents left, but she had put that down to Andy having to work. She was relieved when Cynthia said, "It's nothing serious. Don't even think about it."

"I'm so hopeful about this pregnancy. It's all I think about. I feel much better than I did the other times."

As they left the park, Cynthia said, "Please tell Andy tonight. It'll be easier if he knows, and you'll have his support in eating properly, resting, *et cetera.*"

Andy was overjoyed but also overanxious. He immediately opened the fridge for a bottle of champagne.

"A little won't hurt, will it?"

"I'm going to pass, but you go ahead."

The following morning, he wasn't concerned if Brigitte was up or dressed when he knocked on her door. He had to tell her. She reminded him she'd seen the healing of a health situation in the cards and told him not to worry. His being relaxed would be good for Alice.

Having shared a brownstone with the Harrises during the time of earlier miscarriages, Christophe couldn't continue his anger at Andy any longer when told the good news. He called Andy with his congratulations.

"But you really have to stop drinking and gambling."

"Don't worry, I've got everything under control."

"I think I've heard that before."

By Saturday they were back playing tennis together. They'd shared so many ups and downs in life; their friendship was solid and would mend.

A few weeks later, Brigitte waylaid Andy in the entrance, "Handy, you have a fine eye, and we need your advice." Andy followed her into the apartment and nodded his appreciation of all the floral tributes adorning the small sitting room. Laid on the sofa were five Romeo sized jackets in all colors except red.

"Now, which one should Romeo choose? He can't make up his mind." Romeo's big bloodshot eyes looked up at him saying, "Help me, Handy," as clearly as if he had spoken.

"Juliette has a red helmet and red leather jacket, so it can't be red." Brigitte added.

"Every time I ask him to choose he just walks up and down sniffing each one," Brigitte said to Andy, then turned to Romeo, "Come along, *chéri*, we don't have all day."

"British racing green and a helmet to match. He's a sophisticated dog and will want his wardrobe to be sartorially cool, yet correct," Andy said.

"I knew I could count on you. On another note, Robert wants to invite you and Alice to join us for dinner at Lasserre with Sophie and Jacques, her brother. Jacques is coming for the wedding, of course, and Lasserre is his favorite restaurant."

"Lasserre. What a treat! We've never been."

"I expect they'll be closed in August, so it'll have to be soon. I'll check on Jacques's arrival and let you know."

The night was hot when they walked up the flight of stairs and met in the main room of the famous restaurant. Robert ordered a magnum of Bollinger champagne, and everyone, except Alice, was having a glass while chatting and admiring the orchid-filled dining room with its renowned retractable ceiling. Alice was surprised to see Andy drinking as he had joined her in abstinence ever since she'd told him she was pregnant. But this was a special place and the beginning of wedding festivities.

Jacques looked very like his father and entertained the whole table with stories of his New York experience. With Alice on one side and Brigitte on the other, he managed to keep both ladies interested and amused. From across the table, Andy listened and felt homesick.

Sophie interrupted Jacques, "You won't believe this, but Andy and Alice know Cynthia Maupassant."

"Do we?" asked Alice.

"Yes, you do. That's Cynthia Lecerf, to you. According to Jacques she could've been a drummer, if she hadn't wanted to save the world."

Jacques insisted that it wasn't too late for Cynthia.

"Well, the world's a better place with her as a psychiatric nurse. We don't need any more drummers," Sophie said primly.

"Sophie's just jealous. Cynthia was a natural." As this banter between siblings was going on, Alice noticed that Andy was drinking too fast, like he was making up for lost time. He hadn't had a drop in a month.

"Do you like jazz, Brigitte?" Jacques asked.

"I love it, and on my one and only trip to the States, I went to New Orleans and heard Sweet Emma Barrett sing and play the piano at Preservation Hall. She was a bit past her prime, but it's one of my fondest memories of that trip."

Jacques was impressed, and everyone could see that Brigitte had made a big hit with him.

"I have a great singer in my band, Jill O'Neill. She has the style of a true diva, and I'm changing the name of my band to 'Jacques and Jill'. What do you think?"

"What was the name before?" Brigitte wanted to know.

"'Jacques of Clubs', but no one could remember it."

"I like 'Jacques and Jill', but what if she leaves you?"

"I'm hoping she never will. You'll meet her at the wedding. The whole band's coming to play for you."

It just so happened that Andy was away from the table when the famous ceiling painted with floating nymphs parted drawing diners' eyes to the night sky above. Andy too looked upwards as he was walking back to the table. He lost his direction and stumbled onto a serving station. No harm was done, and he collected himself holding his head high as he took his place between Brigitte and Sophie. But Alice was anxious and decided to keep an eye on him. He continued looking at the sky, throwing back the wine and not joining in the conversation. Alice and Brigitte's eyes met briefly once and both knew what the other thought.

Alice forced herself to join in the happiness of the table while willing Andy to look in her direction, but he resolutely refused. For dessert, Brigitte had preordered passion fruit soufflés for everyone, and for some reason Andy thought it was scrambled eggs. He asked for salt and pepper to be brought and loaded his soufflé with both to the silent horror of the others.

A bit later, just as they'd ordered coffee, a few drops of rain fell into the room before the roof quickly closed. Alice noticed Andy lose all color in his face.

Alice jumped up and rushed to his side. "Andy's not well. He must have eaten something." With Jacques's help Andy made it to the bathroom where he slumped down onto the marble floor.

Jacques stood back looking at Andy. "You haven't eaten anything bad, have you? You're just drunk. Let's get you some fresh air."

Alice couldn't wait outside any longer and pushed the door open into the men's room to find Jacques hauling a protesting Andy to his feet. "You'd better get a taxi, Alice. I'll help you take him home."

"No, I'll take him. Would you please make our excuses to Brigitte and your father? Andrew is not well. Must be something he ate." Andy managed to stagger to the taxi before he passed out, but only just.

It cost a lot to persuade the taxi driver to help Alice haul Andy into their apartment. Alice was so grateful she gave him double what he'd asked. She sat at the end of the bed. "Here I am pregnant. What would it take to make you stop drinking?" she asked aloud in the dark room.

Andy's phone rang. Alice could see it was Billy but decided to let it ring.

The alarm went off at seven. Alice was already up and dressed.

"Call Stan and tell him I'm sick, darlin', please."

"I can't."

"Just this once, please."

She picked up the phone.

"Stan, Andy has food poisoning. He's very sick."

"Have you called the doctor?"

"No. I think the worst is over. He might be in later. He'll call." Alice replaced the phone on the table.

"Thank you." Andy groaned

All this time Andy had not opened his eyes.

"Why do you do it, Andy?"

"I don't know."

"Don't you want to stop?"

"Of course I do."

"Why don't you, then?"

"I wish I knew."

"Last night was embarrassing."

"What happened?"
"You don't want to know."

Alice walked into the hall where her briefcase was standing in its usual place on the floor by the coat closet and took a card out of the front pocket where she kept a few personal items.

She went back to Andy who had rolled onto his side ready to go back to sleep. She made sure he could hear her before placing the card on the pillow.

"Here's a number to call, if you really want to stop. My baby is not going to have a drunk for a father. You'll have to choose."

Walking to work, Alice felt quite light-headed and to her amazement found herself pleased with her decision and rational behavior. She unconsciously placed a protective hand over her baby. The shadow seeping across her marriage ceased to frighten her.

Alice's words had stung. As soon as Andy heard the front door close, he forced himself to make the call. A man called Bert with an American accent answered. After a brief conversation, Andy showered and dressed and took a handful of Advil. He would have two visitors at ten. He had no idea what to expect. The only thing he knew for certain was that he couldn't lose Alice. And another thing, not so certain, was that he might have been hallucinating. Roofs coming off of buildings? Rain inside a restaurant? It was time for some serious help.

CHAPTER 23

A week before the wedding Gladys and Herb arrived with a whoosh, and Alice was placed on one of the thrones where she was watched, monitored and overly cared for. Gladys's big smile had a comforting effect on both Alice and Andy. And Herb's return to the nearby bakery was met with arm-raising joy from behind the counter plus a test on the names of breads and other goodies, much to the consternation of the queuing customers.

The Blanes were surprised and delighted to find neither Alice nor Andy drinking. They were relieved to see real food in the apartment as well as light fixtures, bedside tables and curtains. Paintings hung on the walls, mirrors were installed in the bathrooms and the boxes had been unpacked. The warehouse look had been replaced by Parisian chic.

Patrick Rolland usually closed his salon for the whole month of August and went off to laze by the Mediterranean Sea, but it was *pas possible* to allow all his favorite ladies to celebrate something so important as Brigitte's wedding without his special touch. He took the TGV back to reopen the salon on the day before the wedding. Brigitte, Gladys, Cynthia and Alice had to be steamed and smoothed and polished. Then they had to be coiffed and painted and spritzed, and there was no one in Paris he could rely upon to do the job his way.

The day itself arrived noisily and early in the fifth floor apartment. Andy and Herb thought it better if they breakfasted at La Rotonde. Downstairs, calmness reigned as Brigitte fed Romeo a few milk bones when they returned from their first walk of the day. She sat on the sofa, lit a cigarette and thought about the day ahead. Patrick would come at noon with Giselle to do the make up, hair and help her dress. He said he'd bring sandwiches, and they would take their time. Patrick and Giselle would make sure she was at her very best.

Romeo padded over, and she stroked his head. "What would I have done without you all these years, Romeo" and she told him the day's plans one more time even though he was yawning. "Andy and Alice will pick us up at two and drive to the chateau. Andy has arranged for Gladys and Herb to go with the Lecerfs. The ceremony will start at five in the family chapel. Robert's brother, Jean-Luc, will officiate at the ceremony. I do hope he likes you and me. Robert has told me so much about him. I feel I know him already.

"After the ceremony, there'll be thirty of us for dinner on the terrace and all the doors will be open so we'll hear the harpist playing Robert's Empire harp in the blue drawing room. It's all so thrilling, Romeo! How can you sleep on a day like today?" Brigitte stood and walked around the room trailing her hand along the backs of the chairs. "Jacques's band will play on the *parterre* below the terrace after dinner." She turned and prodded Romeo with her foot. "You and Juliette will love the Jazz. Will you ask her to dance?

Still standing Brigitte gave a laugh when she remembered how long she took to plan the menu. "I think the caterers were a little annoyed. But I liked their idea of a long narrow table with a green and white toile tablecloth and large white linen napkins with lacework edges. Having a long table will leave plenty of room for people to circulate during the cocktail hour and then dance afterwards.

"There's hardly anything except dahlias blooming now in the garden, and Robert laughed when I told him I wanted to use the pink and orange ones for the wedding. He said there wouldn't be nearly enough. So we've added orange roses from the florist. There'll be rose collars for both you and Juliette, so don't ever say I forgot about you on my wedding day."

Slipping into a glamorous *robe de chambre*, she sprayed some Shalimar on Romeo, waking him, much to his disgust, and looked around the small room. "Thank you, God, for this wonderful new happiness." She physically felt the joy as if it were a cloak thrown over her. "Look at the power of love, Romeo. Our lives have been transformed."

The knock at the door heralded the end of her life alone. Lulu crossed the threshold first sporting white lace, and Patrick wearing his brogues with no socks followed pulling a gold suitcase with the tools of his trade. Then came Giselle humming Handel's Wedding March and carrying raspberry *madeleines* from Fauchon and rosé champagne.

It was Patrick who answered a second knock two hours later. "We're almost ready. Come in, Handy."

"You look stunning, Brigitte. So different from the lady I met in January." Andy checked himself. "Not that you didn't look beautiful in January, but today, wow." He held Brigitte at arms' length before kissing her on both cheeks.

Today Brigitte's smile was as big as Gladys's. She had on a cream-colored suit from Nina Ricci with a fascinator they'd made of the same material in her hand. It had a large, stiff ribbon bow, which stood up. Brigitte had worried that it was too trendy for her but was assured by everyone that it was just right, and it was.

"The car's outside," said Andy with a twinkle in his eye, "It's time to go." Andy had refused to divulge to anyone what type of car he had booked. While searching, a stretched Hummer had called out to Andy from the rental website, 'I'm the one, take me,' and he was sorely tempted. But Brigitte's plea, 'Please, Handy, not a Hummer' had proved stronger.

Andy led them to a 1961 black Thunderbird convertible with red leather interior. "This will have to do."

"So beautiful, Handy. I love this car. Thank you." Brigitte gave Andy a hug and kissed Alice who was already standing by the car.

"*Mais,* Handy, the top cannot be down. *Non, non, non! C'est pas possible après* all the time with the hair." Giselle was firm.

Romeo and Lulu dove into the foot wells, and Giselle insisted on sitting in the middle between Patrick and Alice. Once everyone was strapped in, they started the song-filled two-hour drive to the chateau.

In Christophe's car, Gladys, chic in her lilac Armani suit, provided all the conversation for the journey, and they arrived ahead of the Thunderbird. As they pulled into the long drive Gladys said, "Just think Herby, if things had worked out differently this chateau might have been Sugarfoot's."

"How on earth would she ever get to work?" Herb was glad things had worked out as they had.

Cynthia agreed with Herb. "I wouldn't want the responsibility of keeping up a place of this size. Too much work. Far better to be a guest."

As they got out of the car, Gladys wanted to ask Cynthia if she had ever met the ghosts but thought better of it as Sophie was walking towards them with another gentleman.

Sophie embraced her friends Cynthia and Christophe who seemed to know and like the man with her. Herb was worried Sophie might not remember him and Gladys, but of course she did and introduced them to her uncle Jean-Luc who had traveled from his mission in Senegal to officiate at the wedding.

The flower-filled, candle-lit chapel welcomed Brigitte into the la Vallière family. Robert took her hand as she stepped through the door, and together they walked the few paces to the altar where Robert's brother Jean-Luc was waiting. Romeo and Juliette watched with the ghosts from the doorway in complete silence until the end of the ceremony when the parrot whispered, "Hallelujah! Hallelujah! We love you, Brigitte." Somehow Captain knew this was not the moment to make himself known to the assembled guests.

Alice thought the celebration would be a challenge for Andy, and she held his hand as they walked from the chapel to the terrace. When they reached the chateau a white-gloved waiter offered them a tray with a choice between sparkling water and champagne. Andy first passed her a glass of sparkling water and then turned to take a glass for himself. He wanted the champagne but managed to pick up another sparkling water to toast Brigitte and Robert. For a moment he couldn't speak and concentrated on the harp playing in the background, but it wasn't enough. He felt himself giving in. He walked inside reaching for his phone as he went.

His new friend, Bert, answered on the first ring. "Just because you want a drink right now, Andy, doesn't mean you *have* to have one. Think of the consequences, and remember drinking and gambling have *not* worked out well for you so far. And if you take this glass, you know from experience, it will lead to another and another. You told me you want to be the best husband and father that you can possibly be. You can remember what you want, or get drunk tonight and lose the chance to be either. I *know* you can get through the next half an hour without a drink.

Then call me back. I'll keep my phone on."

Andy put his phone back into his pocket, looked at the glass in his hand and went back to Alice. She leaned towards him and tucked her head into his neck and put her arm around his waist.

"Andy!" It was Gladys tugging at his arm. "Isn't that one of the artists you wrote about back in New York?" She was pointing at Junior Viper, who was talking to Sophie. "I recognize him from a photograph in your magazine, next to some contemporary stuff that for the life of me I don't understand. I used to read all your reviews. We have a subscription to *Cool,* you know. "

"Don't let him hear you call his art 'stuff', Gladys. He's my boss now. Come and meet him."

Alice wandered off and found Herb laughing with a very chic lady in front of the hors d'oeuvre buffet holding delicate morsels in their hands.

"I'm going to repeat that, madame. *Salade d'homard aux endives.* Was that okay?"

"Excellent, monsieur. *Parfait.*" And they popped the delicious treats into their mouths and giggled.

"Your turn. Now you say, 'toast with sour cream and caviar'. But it's the same word, that's too easy."

"*Mais délicieux",* and they ate those and laughed again.

Alice left them to it and headed towards Cynthia and Sophie who had their heads together. Alice's loose-fitting silk dress wafted gently as she moved through the crowd.

"What are you two so intent about?"

Cynthia said, "Alice, it's so cool to meet Junior after seeing his paintings in your living room in Brooklyn for all those years. It never occurred to me that he knew Sophie. How do you think his paintings look in the blue *salon*?"

"Are they in there? I haven't been inside yet."

Sophie blushed. "After Andy told me how valuable they are, and here I'd had two of them in my bathroom, I thought we should bring them downstairs and give them pride of place, especially since Junior was coming to the wedding." She glanced over at Junior who was now talking to Andy and Gladys. "Come see the paintings and tell me how you like them, Alice." Sophie stepped into the *grand salon* followed by Alice and Cynthia.

The big canvases hung on either side of the fireplace overlapping the lines of the paneling, the bold colors washing out the centuries old pastel coloring in the rest of the room. Alice caught her breath.

She didn't know what to say and was saved by Junior coming into the room with Andy and Gladys. "Sophie, you've got to get my stuff out of here. Ruins the room." Junior went over and put his arm around Sophie and kissed the top of her head. "I love that they've made it out of the upstairs bathroom, but they'd be better in the entrance hall. Tomorrow I'll help you re-hang them." Gladys made a note to remind Andy that Junior had called his own art 'stuff'.

Robert was passing by and inwardly applauded Junior. He thought they would look wonderful anywhere, anywhere but here.

"This isn't the place for them, but they're a hell of a pair of paintings, Junior." Andy sincerely hoped Junior hadn't thrown the rest away.

"You know, for a long time I thought I could never paint this well again, and I didn't show anyone the paintings I did at Yale. Afraid of comparison. But now I'm ready to show the early work."

When time came for dinner, the guests consulted place cards and took their seats at the long table. Twilight and candles lit the terrace, complementing the brightly colored flowers arranged in a lengthy line of clear glass cubes. Robert whispered in Brigitte's ear, "Dahlias and roses. Symbols of dignity, elegance and a commitment of love and a bond that will last forever."

Brigitte took his hand and kissed his wedding ring.

Andy felt much better once he had some food in him. The soup was spicy hot, yet cold and creamy. It took the edge off his frazzled nerves, and he began to relax and enjoy himself. He was seated between Sophie and a charming friend of Brigitte's who revealed more of the past than Brigitte would have liked. To Andy's great surprise, no wine was being poured into any of the glasses lined up in front of Junior, who was sitting between Sophie and Gladys.

After the fish course was cleared, Andy excused himself for a moment to make another call to his friend. "Bert, I feel okay now. Most people don't drink very much, do they? And, guess what. I think my new boss doesn't drink at all. Call you tomorrow."

Andy was back before anyone noticed he'd gone. He did worry, but only a little bit, about the impression Gladys was making on Junior. He felt a blast of love for Gladys, which also surprised him. She flashed her warm smile at him, and he blew her a kiss. He'd never done that before.

Just as the wedding cake was being served, a rooster crowed loudly from under the table. Conversations stopped as heads went down to see what was there. A bull bellowed above the table making those that did not have their heads down pull back. Robert stood, "Captain, you stop that at once!"

"No," the parrot shrieked and made an elephant's trumpeting sound. The table dissolved into peals of laughter, those acquainted with the family ghosts explaining to the uninitiated.

Brigitte rose to her feet beside Robert and said very calmly, "Captain, can you tone it down a little?" In reply, he squawked, "Party. Party. Party."

Captain then went through his entire repertoire of animal sounds until Jacques's saxophone accompanied by

Jill's singing captured his attention. He flew straight to Jill and perched on her shoulder until his ghostly family lured him away.

Some danced, and everyone laughed as the warm night air suffused them with joy. At midnight the sky erupted in a blaze of fireworks. Andy's phone pinged. He read the few words from Billy, "Eureka, bro. More than our wildest dreams!"

As rockets burst into stars overhead, Olivier rowed his beloved Mathilde silently along the moat in a little green barque. Mathilde was holding on tightly to Captain with one hand to keep him from mischief, and with the other she waved to the terrace. Behind her, running across the lawn was a wild pig being chased by two basset hounds with rose collars and two men, one with a rake and the other with a shovel.

THE END

JANE FOSTER

Foster's first novel, Below Sea Level won the illumination Book Award bronze medal for fiction published in 2013. It was followed in 2015 by Sliding which won the Eric Hoffer Gold Medal Finalist Award for fiction.

Presaging Foster's foray into novel writing were her studies in English Literature and Art History at Finch College in New York City, Following her studies, she worked at Sotheby's for eight years before founding her jewelry design business where she worked closely with famed jeweler, Fred Leighton. Foster is a passionate horticulturist, and two of her gardens are included in the Smithsonian Archives of American Gardens.

Foster currently divides her time between Florida and France.

ANNE YELLAND

Anne Yelland has spent the first half of her life so far in London and the second half living in and around Paris, France. A Psychology graduate and teacher of English as a Foreign language, her early work in copywriting, public relations and government communications opened her eyes to the endless possibilities of writing fiction. Yelland met Foster in a writers' group in Paris and this is her first book.